W9-BDJ-722

Praise for the Inspector DeKok Series by Baantjer

"DeKok is a careful, compassionate policeman in the tradition
of Maigret; crime fans will enjoy this book."
—*Library Journal*

"Baantjer's laconic, rapid-fire storytelling has spun out a
surprisingly complex web of mysteries."
—*Kirkus Review*

"DeKok's maverick personality certainly makes him a
compassionate judge of other outsiders and an astute analyst
of antisocial behavior."
—*The New York Times Book Review*

"It's easy to understand the appeal of Amsterdam police
detective DeKok; he hides his intelligence behind a
phlegmatic demeanor, like an old dog that lazes by the
fireplace and only shows his teeth when the house is
threatened."
—*The Los Angeles Times*

"DeKok's offbeat personality keeps readers interested."
—*Publishers Weekly*

"A major new voice in crime fiction for America."
—*Clues: A Journal of Detection*

"Baantjer seduces mystery lovers. Inspector DeKok is part
Columbo, part Clouseau, part genius, and part imp."
—*West Coast Review of Books*

"... supports the mystery writer's reputation in his native Holland as a Dutch Conan Doyle. His knowledge of esoterica rivals that of Holmes, but Baantjer wisely uses such trivia infrequently, his main interests clearly being detective work, characterization and moral complexity"
—*Publishers Weekly*

"There's no better way to spend a hot or a cold day than with this man who radiates pleasure, adventure and overall enjoyment. A five star rating for this author ..."
—*Clues: A Journal of Detection*

"DeKok's American audiences can delight in his work. Descriptive passages decorate the narrative like glittering red Christmas baubles."
—*Rapport*

Other Inspector DeKok Mysteries

Now Available or Coming Soon

DeKok and Murder by Melody
DeKok and the Death of a Clown
Murder In Amsterdam

DeKok and the Geese of Death

Includes the short story
DeKok and the Grinning Strangler

by

A. C. Baantjer

Translated by H. G. Smittenaar

speck press
denver

Book layout and design by: *Magpie,* magpiecreativedesign.com
Printed and bound in the United States of America

Library of Congress Cataloging-in-Publication Data

Baantjer, A. C.
[De Cock en de ganzen van de dood. English]
DeKok and the geese of death : includes the short story DeKok and the grinning strangler / by A.C. Baantjer ; translated by H.G. Smittenaar.
p. cm.
ISBN 0-9725776-6-1
1. DeKok, Inspector (Fictitious character)--Fiction. I. Title: DeKok and the grinning
strangler. II. Baantjer, A. C. De Cock en de grijnzende wurger. English. III. Smittenaar, H.
G. IV. Title.

PT5881.12.A2D56313 2004
839.3'1364--dc22
2004020102

10 9 8 7 6 5 4 3 2 1

AMSTERDAM

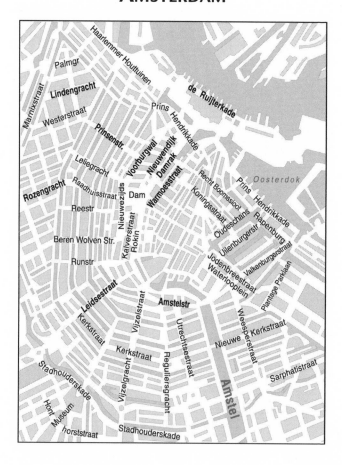

1

"I found the old man dead ... stiff as a salted ... eh, dead. He just fell over when I touched him. It was creepy ... like moving through a nightmare. I just couldn't believe he was gone."

His face twitching, the young man gestured spasmodically with both hands, as if groping for something just out of reach.

"It was eerie," he went on. "I've always been afraid somebody would die right in front of me someday."

Inspector DeKok of the Amsterdam Municipal Police (Homicide) looked at Igor Stablinsky. There was an ironic smile around his mouth as he shook his head.

"I don't get a sense of fear from you," said DeKok.

The young man hesitated. His tongue licked his dry lips and a deep furrow appeared in his forehead.

"You don't get how this could be traumatic?" asked Igor, uncertain about his own credibility. There was a hint of the martyr in his expression and in his voice.

DeKok looked at him evenly. Suddenly the old sleuth's craggy face lost all expression.

"You are hardly traumatized, Igor," he said with a cynical undertone. "No, you are a cool one. You planned to crack Samuel Lion's head open; you had just the right weapon, your crowbar. You had no worries—didn't hesitate for more than a moment. Come on, the old man was dozing in his chair. His back was toward you, Igor. Even had he been awake, he wouldn't have had any warning. He was too deaf to hear you."

Igor Stablinsky leapt out of his chair.

"I didn't kill him," he shrilled. He leaned toward DeKok, his eyes bulging, the cords of his neck constricted. "You hear me? Are you listening? I didn't kill him! Not me! The old man was already dead when I came in."

DeKok regarded him with a mild smile. He was well aware, from previous interrogations, how tenacious Igor Stablinsky could be. Regardless of how damning the evidence, Stablinsky protested his innocence. If the vehemence of his lies convinced no one else, it strengthened his resolve.

DeKok sighed.

"How many more times are you going to burden me with your version of the facts," he asked wearily. "Ten times? Twenty times? It is so tiresome, and I am so very tired. How about telling me the truth, just this one time?"

Igor Stablinsky pressed his lips together so as to avoid saying another word.

"It's the truth," he hissed finally.

A slight pause, then he continued in a calmer, almost normal, tone of voice.

"The absolute, unaltered truth. I found the old man as stiff as a salted cod … as I said."

He fell back into his chair.

"What do you want to hear from me?" he asked defiantly. "A lie? You really want me to tell you I spilled the old guy's brains? Why? Why should I incriminate myself? For the further glory of Inspector DeKok?"

The old inspector sighed. His facial expression, like his posture, sagged a little.

"My glory, as you call it, has nothing to do with it. Look around you—this look like a celebrity tea?" Stablinsky bent close over DeKok's desk.

"Just what *is* in it for you?" he demanded.

DeKok did not take his eyes from his opponent.

"Aside from protecting the public, I'm here to serve justice."

The young man gave the inspector a mocking look.

"Justice … for who?"

DeKok did not answer. He rubbed his lined face with a flat hand while he looked at Stablinsky through spread fingers. He knew this guy was thirty-five years old, but the suspect looked considerably younger. He was almost handsome. The slightly hooked, sharply delineated nose suited the pale narrow face with its slightly protruding cheekbones. But his gray-blue, alert eyes stood a little too close together. Deep set and hooded, they gave a strange expression to the face. The look reminded one of a vulture, closely observing the death throws of its prey.

With another sigh DeKok opened one of the drawers in his desk and took out a blue painted crowbar. It was contained in a narrow bag of clear plastic. The open end of the bag was tied off with a piece of string. The knot of the string was sealed with a piece of lead on which the Shield of the City of Amsterdam was impressed by special pliers. This method of containment maintained the chain of custody. It protected material evidence from incidental fingerprints, as well as preventing interference with any foreign matter on the object.

He placed the covered crowbar on the desk in front of him. He used a pencil to point at a few gray hairs and some blood on the surface of the tool.

"Look, Igor," he said patiently. "The blood evidence alone will leave no doubt old Sam was killed with this crowbar." He cocked his head and one eyebrow at the suspect. "The crowbar is yours, is it not, Igor," he added.

The young man closed his eyes for a moment. Then he opened them slowly.

"Not my property," he growled. "I have never seen the crowbar before. How many times do I have to repeat myself?"

DeKok sighed again, as if bored. He searched in a stack of reports on the corner of his desk.

"Here," he continued, unperturbed. "I have a statement from a Mrs. Brooyman, Samuel Lion's housekeeper. According to her statement she was in bed in the room next door and thought she heard a thud. Startled, she rose immediately, and threw on a robe. When she opened the door of the living room she saw you bending over Samuel Lion's body. You looked up, paused for a moment, and then fled through the open window."

Stablinsky shrugged his shoulders.

"I'm sure that's correct," he said. "You don't have to rehash it. I know about that statement. I even admitted I was there."

DeKok did not break stride. He continued, ignoring the interruption.

"In light of our previous experiences with you and the clever manipulations of your lawyer, we made absolutely sure to get a positive identification from the line-up. The witness picked you out of four different groups of men, all your size and build. That's four lineups."

There was a hint of admiration in DeKok's voice as he glanced from the report to the suspect.

"Mrs. Brooyman was positive ... adamant. She swore a mistake was out of the question—she would recognize *you* out of thousands."

Stablinsky fidgeted in his chair, but DeKok ignored it.

"And I'm not surprised," he said, "... once somebody has seen that vulture face of yours, they're not likely to forget it."

Suddenly an angry light sparked in Stablinsky's eyes.

"That's an insult, DeKok," he spat out. "I don't have to take it! There's no need to get personal. What's my face got to do with it? You don't hear me saying your face belongs on some punchy, over-the-hill boxer ... some sleep-deprived geezer who's on a perpetual binge."

The inspector laughed heartily.

"You're right, Igor," he admitted. "I'm sorry. There was no need to get personal. 'Vulture face' is such an unrefined term. Maybe it was a cheap shot." He made an apologetic gesture. "But you have only yourself to blame. Your insistent denial is enough to try the patience of a saint. I have never claimed saintliness. You can keep on saying that white is black, or vice versa, but repeating a lie doesn't make it true. I just want to talk to you, Igor. But your attitude makes it impossible to have a normal conversation."

DeKok paused and put the report back on the stack.

"Personally," he went on in a reasonable tone of voice, "I'm convinced you savagely murdered Samuel Lion. I am equally sure you brutalized the widow Linshot seventeen months ago. While the ink dried on her death certificate, you took off with the old lady's savings."

Stablinsky smirked.

"It's on you. You're the one who let me walk, Inspector."

DeKok nodded slowly.

"Lack of evidence," he admitted, regret in his voice. "It wouldn't have served your interests to confess. In fact, it would have been senseless. A confession or guilty plea would likely result in you spending the prime of your life in prison. At the time you had no reputation as a violent perpetrator. Your record was clean, so to speak, other than misdemeanors."

DeKok smiled ruefully.

"All we knew about you was that you weren't a player. You'd committed a few minor burglaries, preferring to target homes of the elderly. We had nothing to link you to murder in a Court of Law."

DeKok fell silent and took a deep breath.

"But this time," he said, "this time it's different. Now I have clear, concrete evidence; no judge in Holland, no matter how lenient, will let you off. That's why contradiction is useless. On the contrary, it's merely foolish."

Stablinsky's voice began to get shrill again.

"I decide what's foolish," he said defiantly.

DeKok pursed his lips and shook his head.

"It was foolish to bash in the head of a defenseless old man—ruthless and messy. Samuel Lion's murder was the act of a maniac, a mental case."

Again Stablinsky jumped to his feet.

"When is this going to stop? How long are you going to keep this up?" He screamed, foam on his lips. "I know my rights." He brought his right hand to his lips, licked the tips of his fingers, then raised his hand. "I am swearing to you, DeKok, I am no murderer. On my mother's grave I did NOT kill that old man."

He shrugged his shoulders. It was a nonchalant gesture.

"I'm not impressed," he stated calmly. He looked up at Stablinsky. "As *my* old mother used to say: 'Who swears easily, lies easily.'" He pointed at the chair in front of his desk. "Sit down, Igor," he said sternly with a hint of irritation in his voice. "You're getting on my nerves."

Reluctantly, Stablinsky regained his seat. DeKok rummaged briefly in his desk drawer and held up a small, brown-leather book. It was an engagement calendar.

"In addition to the statement from Mrs. Brooyman and the crowbar with the hair and blood of the victim, guess what? I also ran across this agenda while searching your home. It was in the inside pocket of one of your sportcoats."

DeKok opened the little book and rifled the pages.

"In here," he continued, "I found a number of names and addresses. Among them were the names and addresses of Mrs. Linshot and that of Samuel Lion. I presume you have a reasonable explanation for that?"

Stablinsky moved in his chair.

"Those are simply the names and addresses of acquaintances."

It even sounded lame to Stablinsky. DeKok smiled to himself.

"Well," he said, "I, for one, am glad I don't belong to your circle of acquaintances. Some have a tendency to come to unfortunate ends."

He flipped some pages, looking for the right one.

"We checked the list, you see, my partner Vledder and I. You might say we checked it twice." he grinned without mirth. "Those who are still alive, are all people of means … *older* people of means." he glanced at the young man.

"What is your plan, Igor?" he inquired gently. "Were you going to try and wipe them out at your leisure? What exactly is your problem … do you have a special hatred for rich old people?"

Igor Stablinsky answered sullenly.

"There is no plan. I repeat, I am no murderer."

"Do you mind if I feel compelled to differ with you?"

"I have nothing against old people."

DeKok grinned again without a trace of pleasure.

"Unless, of course, they're worth a bundle."

Stablinsky looked sharply at the man on the other side of the desk. His cheeks were turning red and his steely eyes narrowed as if to hide a murderous gleam.

DeKok placed the agenda on the desk and leaned back in his chair. There was a pensive look on his face.

"What strikes me as more than coincidence," he said slowly, thoughtfully, "is the fact both victims ... Mrs. Linshot and Old Sam ... were approached from behind by their assailant or assailants." He cocked his head at Stablinsky. His stare captured the eyes of the young man. "I'd lay odds you don't have the guts to let even a frail victim look you in the eyes."

A phone rang on the credenza behind DeKok' desk. The old inspector shoved the agenda back in the drawer and turned his chair halfway to pick up the phone. The moment he brought the phone to his ear, a piercing cry cut through the background noise.

"DeKok!"

It was Vledder's voice.

DeKok turned facing the desk. In an instant he realized the danger. He bent to the side, simultaneously pushing himself away from the desk. The casters on the chair did the rest, rolling him out of harm's way. The phone smacked the floor in the process.

With a deafening crash the crowbar, still in its plastic bag, hit the edge of the desk, inches from where DeKok's head had been. As Vledder wrestled Stablinsky, DeKok picked up the phone and yelled into the mouthpiece.

"Hold, please," he said loudly.

He held the phone as a few officers from neighboring desks helped drag Stablinsky toward the door of the large detective room. Then he continued the phone conversation, struggling to control a slight tremble in his voice.

After Igor Stablinsky, yelling and screaming, had been led away by a couple of uniformed constables, DeKok replaced the phone on the credenza. He was ashen and looked shaken. His hand traveled over the desktop. The metal edge of the desk had a big dent. He looked at Vledder's worried face.

"Thanks, my boy," he said quietly.

"I just happened to come in," smiled the young inspector.

"I was careless," admitted DeKok. "I shouldn't have left that crowbar in plain view. And I should never have interviewed him without cuffs. He smiled briefly. "... sorry I didn't wait for you." He took a deep breath and exhaled slowly. His heart again beat normally. He smiled again as he looked at Vledder.

"Maybe now we can remove this credenza thing *and* the phone from behind my desk. It is too much of a distraction. Put the phone back where it was, on the desk, and give me room."

Vledder looked solemn. DeKok gave him a reassuring grin.

"I know it's not the fault of the phone. Even though I was fully aware I should never turn my back on Igor, the sound of the phone startled me into making a thoughtless move."

Vledder straddled a chair in front of DeKok's desk.

"Did he confess?"

DeKok shook his head.

"I think he'd sooner die a slow death."

Vledder made an impatient gesture.

"What he did to you was attempted murder. Isn't that a kind of confession? At least it proves that Igor Stablinsky is capable of murder ... and ready to ambush a victim or anyone who gets in his way."

DeKok did not answer at once. He rubbed his hand between his neck and his collar as if to get some air. Absentmindedly he noticed he was clammy. His underarms were wet with sweat.

"As evidence in the cases of Mrs. Linshot and Sam Lion, it's worthless. Even a so-so lawyer would explain the attack on me any number of ways. Igor isn't dumb and his lawyer is more than competent. Odds are the two of them will manage to concoct something. I wouldn't be surprised if they come up with an impressive complaint."

"Against you?"

"Yes."

"On what grounds?"

"Oh, excessive force, for instance."

Vledder looked incredulous.

"Did you hit him?"

DeKok laughed.

"Of course not. I'm smarter than that, I hope. I did not lay a finger on him." He shrugged his shoulders. "But a complaint like that does not require any basis in truth."

Vledder seemed confused.

"No basis of truth?" he repeated. "But a false accusation is punishable by law."

DeKok grinned broadly.

"Not if the complaint is against a police officer." It

sounded cynical. "I've never heard of anyone being convicted for falsely accusing a police officer. That seems to be permissible in Holland."

"Did you make Igor angry?"

DeKok stared into the distance while he let the conversation run through his memory. He had an uncanny ability to recall the words, facial expressions, and gestures of past interviews. Then he shook his head.

"No," he said thoughtfully. "At times the conversation was somewhat vehement. We were not exactly exchanging pleasantries, but I don't think there was real anger involved. Stablinsky feigned anger, maybe."

"So?" pressed Vledder.

"As you know, it's not always easy to remain completely calm during an interrogation. There are always moments when emotions threaten to get the best of you. It goes with the territory. And Igor Stablinsky is a very clever suspect. That stubborn, stupid denial undermines self-control. Like any interrogator, I grow impatient. Then my temper flares. This time I pursued the line of questioning, because I felt he was coming unglued just enough to confess. Just then the phone started to ring."

Vledder gave him a thoughtful look.

"Who was on the phone?"

DeKok grimaced.

"That's what's so odd," he said. "It was a woman, an older woman. She wanted to know if I knew anything about her geese."

"Geese?"

"That's what she said."

"Who was the woman? Do we have a name?"

"Yes," said DeKok, "it was a Mrs. Bildijk."

Vledder looked surprised.

"Bildijk? From along the Amstel?"

"Yes."

"Her name and address are in Stablinsky's agenda."

DeKok slapped his forehead.

"Of course, with all the commotion I did not make the connection right a way. Let's find out more about the good lady."

2

Both inspectors were seated in the old VW Beetle. Vledder was driving. DeKok sprawled his rangy frame as far as possible in the cramped little passenger seat. They passed the dam, the center of Amsterdam; passed the pier with the excursion boats. They crossed the bridge on the way out of town. A dense, dark gray cloud cover hid the sun. Drizzle started hesitantly and then it began to rain decisively. A layer of small water bubbles began to obscure the greasy windshield. Vledder turned on the windshield wipers.

DeKok seemed fascinated by the movement of the wipers. Their slow sweeping motion was mesmerizing. It seemed to soothe him. He shoved his dilapidated little hat deeper over his eyes and sank further into the seat, until he was almost sitting on his back. The knees of his lanky legs braced him against the dashboard.

Vledder looked aside.

"What's going to happen with Stablinsky," he inquired.

DeKok shook his head as if to clear it, banishing the lull of the rain and the hum of the engine. There wouldn't be time for a nap—he sat up, straightening his large frame.

"Tomorrow morning he'll be officially charged by the judge advocate."

"You think they'll even get a conviction?"

"Sure. All his denials aren't going to do him any good.

The evidence is circumstantial, but there is plenty of it."

"That assault on you? I noticed you left it out and I wanted to ask you about that."

He did not answer at once.

Vledder usually took care of all the paperwork concerning their investigations. DeKok had always refused to use a typewriter. He was momentarily vindicated when the last remaining typewriter was relegated to a dank corner in the basement of Warmoes Street. But the advent of computers failed to change DeKok. If anything, the senior inspector grew even more reluctant to use a keyboard. In the beginning of his career all reports were written with pen and ink. The mechanization of the process made it all too hasty. Deliberation and hard work were paramount, so far as he was concerned. Vledder went with the flow. He had worked out a special template for writing reports. He could put out almost any report in a minimum of time by using prepared paragraphs and sub-routines he had stored in the memory of his computer. DeKok could care less how Vledder did it. He refused to acquaint himself with all those electronic aids; however, he was quick enough to accept the benefits of the shortcuts Vledder had developed. He no longer insisted on laboring over his reports, handwriting them in pen and ink. He gave his thoughts, verbally, or in the form of cryptic notes to Vledder. He hid a sly smile when the bureaucracy applauded "his" reports.

"Well," repeated Vledder, "why would you leave it out of the report?"

"I decided it was a 'non-event'—irrelevant to the case."

"You have to be kidding. You almost ended up with that crowbar buried in your skull." Vledder tried to disguise his aggravation.

DeKok shrugged.

"It was my own fault. I should never have given him an opening."

"Right," said Vledder sarcastically. "You happen to walk in front of a loaded gun. Of course, the shooter chooses to pull the trigger as you pass by. He gets off the hook, because why? Because you put yourself in his sights?"

DeKok shrugged, deciding to ignore the hint of sarcasm Vledder certainly had not meant.

"I left the crowbar where he could grab it and then turned away."

"But that's my point," said Vledder, exasperation in his voice. "He made a choice. He surely did not have license to break your head. That's pure nonsense. If he had done it to me, I would have …"

DeKok interrupted him with a gesture. Carefully he fished a peppermint out of a breast pocket and studied it. Then he spoke.

"I knew Igor Stablinsky had killed at least twice with a crowbar," he explained patiently. "Please keep in mind that neither victim was able to look at him. I am a senior inspector here. In spite of my years on the force, I turned my back on a predator who ambushes his prey. Not to mention his weapon of choice sat there, just within his reach. For someone experienced, it was just idiotic. And I do not want anyone to suffer for my stupidity."

Vledder gave the steering wheel an angry slap.

"That's convoluted reasoning, if I ever heard it."

"You think so?"

The younger inspector nodded vehemently.

"Totally insane. Your judgment may have faltered, but the responsibility isn't yours. He chose to grab the crowbar … with every intention of killing you."

DeKok rubbed the back of his neck and popped the peppermint into his mouth. He chewed for a while before he answered.

"If I provide an opportunity for a thief to steal from me, I bear some of the responsibility. I gave Stablinsky the opportunity to act, knowing perfectly well he would leap at the chance." He sighed deeply. "At best it was blatant thoughtlessness on my part."

Vledder would not let up.

"Nonsense," he said. "That's not a reasonable argument. That says we would have to keep all criminals forever behind bars. Setting them free would give them the opportunity to commit additional criminal acts."

DeKok nodded thoughtfully.

"There's something in what you say. No doubt, as far as certain criminals are concerned, everyone in the justice system should be more aware of his responsibilities. For instance: the lives of many innocent victims could be spared if it were harder for convicted murderers to get parole, or light sentences."

"Huh?"

"Oh, yes. There are many examples of that. I remember Jan Vries, for instance. He was convicted for a serial armed robbery. After he was set free, he murdered an entire family … mother, father, and three children. When they returned him to the sanitarium, he held up his hand and spread his fingers. 'Five murders because you swore I was sane again,' he told the psychiatrist."

"Really?"

"Yes, really," answered DeKok who was getting wound up. "Oh, we're quick to give stiff sentences to thieves, swindlers, and the like. I recently read about some cases in

America. Some bookkeeper or other had embezzled a large amount from a company. He got twelve years and a fine in the hundreds of thousands of dollars. The same judge later sentenced a guy to eighteen months for killing his wife. You see the white-collar thief is locked away for twelve years so he cannot steal again any time soon. But the murderer is free to kill again after just eighteen months. In a topsy-turvy system, crimes against property are treated as more heinous than those that destroy human life. You tell me if that's not creating opportunities."

Vledder growled and remained silent.

They eventually reached the outskirts of town and followed the left bank of the river Amstel. Amsterdam was named after a dam that had been built on the river some twelve hundred years earlier. They passed a stretch of condemned houseboats that blighted the landscape and obscured the view. But after a bend in the river, they saw the landscape in its somber splendor. The heavy rainfall of the last few days had swollen the river to the point that a slight breeze threw ripples and wavelets over the banks. A number of windmills were visible that took full advantage of the light breeze and were engaged in bringing the water down to a more manageable level. DeKok's mood turned pensive. He reflected ruefully that there were probably some enormous steam and electrical pumps engaged in the task of the windmills. Sooner or later all the windmills would disappear from this landscape.

His thoughts drifted back to Stablinsky. He felt the case was not yet closed. He was almost certain his path would cross Stablinsky's again, perhaps soon. The sound of the crowbar hitting his desk echoed in his mind.

His usually friendly face changed into a mask of steel. He pressed his lips together into a narrow line. Stablinsky would never get a second shot, he decided, grimly.

He looked at Vledder who clearly was still occupied with his thoughts on crime and punishment.

"Do you remember if Mrs. Bildijk's name and address appeared in Igor's agenda in the same group with those of the two victims?"

Vledder shook his head without taking his eyes off the road.

"No, she was mentioned on a different page, in a different color ink. Somehow I got the impression he entered her particular name and address in the agenda when he first started to use it. Perhaps she was an early target. What I'm saying is he intended her as a victim prior to making the rest of the list. Like the others, though, Mrs. Bildijk is practically defenseless. She's an invalid, who uses a wheelchair. She seems to be a rich and, above all, an eccentric old lady."

"How do you know that?"

Vledder smirked.

"I've known it for a while. As soon as we obtained Igor's notebook, her name was the first we investigated. I also checked with the local police station. She lives in the Twenty-third Precinct."

"And?"

"They recognized her name. As a matter of fact they know her very well. She's one of their favorite cranks. She often calls just to complain."

"What about?"

"Mostly she gripes about inadequate surveillance. The Twenty-third isn't vigilant enough for her. She insists a patrol car stop by her property at least five times per night."

"That's a bit excessive, isn't it?"

Vledder nodded.

"The comissaris of that precinct definitely saw it that way. But I wouldn't underestimate her tenacity. In addition to the nagging, she threatened to inform some highly placed officials. The local commissaris finally buckled. He promised a patrol car would check at least four times per night."

"And that stopped the complaints?"

"Yes and no. One time a car drove by only three times. Sure enough, she was on the phone first thing the next morning. It appeared the old lady stayed awake at night to keep a record each time she saw (or didn't see) a patrol car."

DeKok laughed.

"But why?"

Vledder shrugged.

"Mrs. Bildijk is convinced someone is after her life as well as her possessions. She's also upset about the lack of attention shown by the local station. She wanted a 'real' inspector to look after her interests." He glanced at DeKok. "That's why she called you, I think."

DeKok shoved his hat as far back on his head as it would go, without falling off. He opened the glove compartment and found a long-forgotten toffee. As he slowly unwrapped the sweet he spoke.

"She picked a particularly unfortunate time to call."

They continued in silence, only broken by the rough sound of the engine and sucking noises made by DeKok as he savored his aged toffee.

Suddenly DeKok looked around and gently poked Vledder in the side.

"Are you sleeping with your eyes wide open?"

Vledder looked confused.

"How's that?"

DeKok gestured at the landscape.

"We're way past the outskirts of Amsterdam. You simply passed the Bildijk property. Straight ahead are the first houses of Oldkerk."

They parked the police VW on a narrow shoulder, got out and proceeded on foot. The wind and rain were reaching gale force. DeKok pulled up the collar of his raincoat and pulled his hat deeper over his eyes.

'Happy Lake' was written in gilded letters above the wrought-iron gate. The gate was painted black and securely anchored to two tall, brick pillars. A high wrought-iron fence extended from the pillars in both directions. The visual impact was institutional and forbidding.

Behind the gate a gravel path meandered across the manicured lawn, disappearing between tall hedges of purple rhododendron.

DeKok looked at the heavy steel bolts that secured the gate and realized the gate was not locked. He pushed against one half of the gate, gradually applying more force. Slowly the gate opened. At least one rusty hinge screeched ominously.

As if in answer to the noise, two gaggles of white geese instantly appeared from between the hedges. They spread their wings at a dead run, as if to take flight. They stretched their long necks, uttering hostile hissing sounds.

For a moment DeKok seemed perplexed. Then he hastily backed out of the gate, pulling it shut as he went.

Vledder stepped aside and laughed.

"Afraid of birds?" he asked mockingly.

"Yes," answered DeKok curtly. "Those birds can kill a man."

"Really?" Vledder was skeptical.

DeKok did not respond, but watched an elderly man who had appeared behind the geese. He was wearing wooden shoes and carried a long stick. When he came nearer he threatened the geese with the stick. They dispersed from the gate. The hissing stopped, but the birds fixed their little eyes on the intruders, remaining fully alert.

"Whadda you want?"

There was a sullen tone in the old man's hoarse voice.

DeKok flashed his most winning smile.

"My name is DeKok," he said pleasantly. "DeKok with ... eh kay-oh-kay." He pointed a thumb over his shoulder at Vledder. "This is my colleague, Vledder. We're police officers from Warmoes Street Station."

"Police?"

DeKok nodded.

"Mrs. Bildijk called us on the phone. She wanted to talk." With a hesitant gesture he pointed at the two flocks of birds, silent participants in the conversation. "About, eh ... about her geese."

The man rubbed his nose with the back of hand and snorted.

"Damn geese," he growled, disdain in his voice. "They're filthy, rotten beasts, all of them. If you don't use a stick to keep them from you, they'll tear the clothes right off you. They try to trip you, you know. And once they have you on the ground, watch out! If they hit you with their beaks at the end of those long necks, it's like being hit with hammers. Besides, nobody can train them. But she wanted geese."

He shook his head. "Dogs … dogs weren't good enough for her, nossir. Geese it had to be."

DeKok studied the old man. He looked to be about in his sixties. His skin was wrinkled and weathered. But his gray hair was still thick, and his brown eyes were alert and intelligent.

"You … you work here?"

The old man snorted once more.

"Work?" He shook his head. "I can't call it work. I am more like a serf, completely at the mercy of a mad woman's whim."

DeKok listened carefully to the tone of voice.

"You mean, Mrs. Bildijk."

The old man did not answer. He placed a calloused hand on the gate and pulled it open.

"I'll show you the way. Stay close to me."

He walked ahead of them. His wooden shoes made a crunching sound, as if to pulverize the fine gravel on the path. As the geese tried to close in again, he brandished his stick like a weapon. They scattered, protesting in a cacophony of honking.

The gravel path became wider as they reached the stoop in front of the mansion. The stoop was built with bluestone risers and marble steps. The house itself looked like a small palace with large windows and marble lintels over the door and windows. To the right was a coach house in the same style. There seemed to be a floor over the barn space. The old man pointed with his stick.

"That's where I live and sleep … they won't take me away until one of us, she or I, dies."

They climbed the steps of the stoop. To one side the space between steps was filled with concrete. The resultant ramp was rough and certainly too steep for a wheel chair.

The old man leaned towards the two police officers.

"Let's hope she isn't asleep," he rasped. "At this time of the day she often takes a nap—before she rests, she locks everything."

The old man's wooden shoes resounded on the steps. Vledder and DeKok followed. At the top of the steps the old man halted. He placed one hand under his chin and stood in thought. Finally he turned around, a deep crease in his forehead.

"What was that again … DeKok and … Vledder?"

DeKok nodded.

"From Warmoes Street Station," he confirmed.

The old man turned toward the door and opened it slowly.

"One moment," he said. "I'll announce you."

His hoarse voice suddenly acquired a tone of fear as well as humility. He stepped out of his wooden shoes and left them in front of the door. He walked inside on thick black socks. After a few minutes he reappeared.

"Follow me," he beckoned.

He led them down a wide, marble corridor. Near the end, on the right, he opened a door and made an inviting gesture.

Vledder and DeKok entered a stark, sparsely furnished room. In the center, as if on a throne, a tall, severe looking woman was seated. She turned her head toward the door as the cops entered. DeKok estimated her age in the mid-fifties. Her black hair was caught in a chignon, fastened with a heavy tortoise comb at the back of her head.

DeKok approached with Vledder close behind.

Suddenly the old sleuth halted. His glance went over her face ... the sharply delineated nose, the somewhat wide, protruding cheeks. He looked at her eyes. They were deep set, almost hooded ... just a little too close together. He drew in his breath.

"Igor," he murmured, "Igor Stablinsky."

3

The old man bowed in deference, his hand on the doorknob.

"Will there be anything else, Madam?"

Mrs. Bildijk dismissed him with a wave.

"You may go, Willem," she said evenly. She turned toward DeKok and asked in a different tone of voice: "Did you say something?"

The old inspector smiled.

"No, I didn't say anything. That is … not really. I was just thinking out loud."

She cocked her head at him.

"And I may not share your thoughts?" she wheedled.

DeKok hesitated. He gave her a searching look.

"Your face … for a moment it reminded me of a man who is suspected of having murdered two elderly people."

There was a hint of a smile on her face.

"That does not sound a bit flattering."

Apologetically, DeKok shrugged and spread his hands in a gesture of helplessness.

"I realize that," he said. "But the similarity in appearance is striking. Please believe me. A murderer can look quite attractive, especially if looks combine with a winning personality."

"Misleading?"

"Indeed."

"And who is this murderer who resembles me?"

"Igor Stablinsky."

Mrs. Bildijk shrugged her shoulders in dismissal.

"Stablinsky," she said slowly. "The name means nothing to me."

DeKok gave her a friendly smile.

"I hardly expected that." His voice was reassuring. "I've encountered a resemblance like that numerous times in my career. Most of the time it's sheer coincidence."

He pulled off his wet raincoat, folded it inside out, and placed it over the arm of a chair. He placed his old hat on top of the raincoat. Then he shoved another chair closer to Mrs. Bildijk and sat down. Vledder followed suit.

Mrs. Bildijk waved a hand.

"Willem should have taken your coats," she said. "He must have forgotten. He's getting old and moody. He's no longer as dedicated as he used to be. On the contrary, he's been downright arrogant and impudent, ever since I ordered his dogs destroyed."

DeKok's eyebrows rippled. There is no other word for it. DeKok's eyebrows could take on a life of their own, moving in ways not expected or even assumed possible. DeKok always seemed unaware of the phenomenon. Vledder was always on the lookout for it and liked to study the faces of the people who beheld the extraordinary behavior of DeKok's eyebrows. This time he did not see it happen, but deduced from Mrs. Bildijk's expression that she had clearly seen it. She looked amazed, maybe incredulous.

"Why," asked DeKok sternly, "did you have his dogs killed?"

Mrs. Bildijk, still bemused by DeKok's eyebrows, answered sharply. Perhaps more sharply than she had intended.

"Willem spoiled them." She softened her tone somewhat. "He always spoils dogs he is supposed to be handling … it wasn't any different with those useless Alsatian Shepherds." Her tone became more shrewish as she continued. "They were lazy, stupid, fat animals. They ate almost three pounds of meat every day."

DeKok thought about his own boxer, the fifth of a series of boxers he had owned. One of his regrets had always been that dogs do not live long enough and the loss of each of his companions had always been heart breaking. The thought that someone would kill dogs because they ate too much, disturbed him. He was sensitive on the subject of dogs.

"Was that the only reason," he asked evenly.

She snorted.

"No, they were too friendly."

"Too friendly? Surely that's no reason to kill them."

"Friendly," she repeated. "I do not keep dogs to get fat and lazy. They earn their keep by guarding my property."

"And they did not do that?"

"No, they did not. Whenever a stranger entered the gate, the dogs would greet them with wagging tails."

DeKok swallowed some sharp retorts. He had his own ideas about the relationship between people and animals. But this was not the time.

"So, that is when you decided to get geese?"

She nodded.

"Exactly … geese. You must have heard about the geese that saved Rome from being overrun by the Gauls. Geese are excellent guardians. In groups they can be dangerous to intruders as well. They are territorial, you know, and properly rationed they will defend their turf to the death. No guard dog can top that."

"Rationed?"

"Yes, you must not feed them too much. That way they become even more aggressive, in order to protect their food supply."

"Vicious, would be a more accurate description."

"If you like."

"And you need these vicious guardians?"

Mrs. Bildijk lowered her head.

"I … eh … I'm afraid."

"Of what?"

Her sallow face turned ashen. The light make-up seemed to separate from her skin. It was strange to see how her demeanor changed. It was as if she suddenly became another person. Her hands resting on the armrests of the chair trembled.

"That … that I don't know," she said softly. "It isn't specific, but I feel something is going to happen to me … soon."

DeKok did not press her.

"During our rather abruptly interrupted telephone conversation you told me you wanted to talk about your geese."

Mrs. Bildijk nodded. Slowly she regained her composure.

"I know this is actually not your precinct. But, to be honest, I have little faith in the personnel in my precinct. You, on the other hand, have a very good reputation. That's why I called you."

DeKok ignored the compliment. He was instinctively suspicious of people who used expressions such as 'to be honest' or 'to be frank.' To a career cop, they incriminated themselves for all the times they did lie.

"Why do you need us here to discuss your geese?"

Mrs. Bildijk pointed at her wheelchair standing nearby.

"An invalid is so helpless and dependent," she whined.

DeKok did not take his eyes off her.

"Again Mrs. Bildijk, what's the problem with your geese?" he repeated.

Mrs. Bildijk did not answer at once. The tips of her fingers touched her neck.

"I'm afraid they're being poisoned."

"By whom?"

"Willem."

DeKok showed surprise.

"That old man?"

She nodded slowly.

"I know he recently bought a supply of strychnine."

The old man looked first at DeKok and then at Vledder. His glance went from one to the other a few times before he spoke.

"Strychnine?" he said, amazement in his voice. "Of course, I bought strychnine. I was almost out. I just had another can delivered. It's the only effective way to get rid of moles. They plague us here. They come from the meadows behind us. The farmer does not care, but they ruin the lawns." His stocking feet stomped on the floor. "And down here in the coach house, I've got rats."

DeKok nodded his understanding.

"You fight moles and rats with strychnine."

The man picked up a pipe from the table and emptied it in an ashtray by tapping it against his hand.

"Yes, I've tried other things, but strychnine gives me the best results."

"You don't feel it is overkill?"

The old man shrugged his shoulders.

"Of course it's dangerous, so I handle it very carefully. During the holidays, when the nephews and nieces are here with their children, I keep it under lock and key." He grinned. "The little ones will get into everything." He smiled tenderly. With his pipe he pointed out the window. "They'd rather be here than in the big house."

"Why?" asked DeKok.

Willem did not answer at once. He took a copper tobacco jar from the table and started to fill his pipe slowly and methodically.

"She doesn't like children," he said after a while. "She has no patience with them."

"You're talking about Mrs. Bildijk?"

The man ignored the question. For a moment Vledder was reminded of DeKok's ability to ignore questions as if no one had asked. Willem showed the same bland indifference.

"She never had children of her own," continued Willem hoarsely. "And the Lord knows Mr. Bildijk would have liked children. Squire Iwert was a very caring gentleman ... so patient. It's just too bad he died relatively young. If he had lived, everything would have been different. But he contracted some sort of disease. He just wasted slowly away."

DeKok sensed the undertone.

"You held him in high regard?"

The old man nodded slowly, pensively.

"He was the only reason I stayed on. I was little more than a gardener. But as he lay dying he called me to his side. 'Willem,' he said, 'stay with Isolde. She needs you.' Well, I promised him I would stay."

He paused, lost in thought. After a while, DeKok spoke a question.

"You regret your promise now?"

The old man shook his head.

"Only fools have regrets. At the time of decision, a man is supposed to know what he's doing."

"And you knew." It was not a question.

DeKok received a sad smile in return. Willem pointed at the surroundings: the bare, planked floor, the plain, pine furniture, the rattan chairs, the faded, peeling wallpaper.

"Obviously, it didn't make me wealthy."

"Who said anything about getting rich?"

The old man looked at the pipe in his hands.

"Squire Iwert told me I would be richly rewarded in his will."

"And?"

"But first she …" He did not finish the sentence, but replaced the filled pipe on the table. Slowly he raised his head and met DeKok's eyes with unabashed curiosity.

"Did she send you to speak with me?"

DeKok did not find it necessary to lie.

"Yes," he said.

Because of the geese?"

"Exactly."

A faint grimace played around Willem's lips.

"Well, now you know. I have plenty of strychnine."

They drove back to Amsterdam at a leisurely pace. The rain had stopped, but banks of heavy cumulus clouds drifted against the blue sky. The gray melancholy lifted and sunlight danced over the rippling water of the Amstel. Subconsciously both Vledder and DeKok noticed the level of the water had already noticeably diminished. The windmills had done their work as they had for hundreds of years.

DeKok slid down in his seat and thought about the interviews at Happy Lake. The name seemed a cruel misnomer. He couldn't shake a feeling more of foreboding than gloom. There was a strange, ambivalent relationship between the old woman and her old gardener. Mrs. Bildijk and Willem were ruled by passions and secrets no outsider could fathom. One thing DeKok could discern was the tension between the two. He sensed an explosion in the offing. The elder inspector searched his memory for similar situations from his long career, but could not recall anything quite like it.

Vledder looked at him briefly.

"How did Mrs. Bildijk know her gardener had ordered a new supply of strychnine? She could hardly be expected to search the coach house. I don't think she could have made it on her own."

DeKok thought for a moment.

"I imagine she paid the bill," he said after a brief pause.

Vledder looked surprised.

"You mean to tell me," he exclaimed. "She just read the invoice and then paid the bill—no questions asked."

"That's exactly what I mean."

Vledder grinned.

"But then there's no secret, no hidden motive. The old man wasn't hiding anything."

DeKok looked thoughtful.

"But that does not change the fact that strychnine is a deadly weapon."

Vledder remained silent. They had reached the inner city and he needed all his attention to maneuver the old Volkswagen through the heavy traffic. The narrow streets and quays along the canals were never really intended for motorized traffic. The thousands of bicycles did not make it any easier. In an instant a truck careened toward them—Vledder floored the gas, turning sharply into Half Moon Alley. The tires screeched, as they barely escaped colliding with the truck.

"Cool down," growled DeKok. "I don't want to miss out on my pension this way. You could have cracked an egg between our car and that truck. Whew."

"Well, it was either that, or have him smack into us head on."

DeKok grunted.

Eventually they reached the station house on Warmoes Street.

Vledder parked the car and they entered together.

As they passed the desk of Meindert Post, the watch commander raised a hand.

"DeKok!" he yelled, although DeKok was barely three feet away.

DeKok stopped and turned toward the desk.

"Did you say something, Meindert?" he asked.

For a moment the sergeant looked at him.

"Igor Stablinsky has escaped," he said, still at the same volume as before.

DeKok simply waited for further information, but Vledder could not resist the obvious question.

"Escaped?" he asked.

Post handed them a report.

"Escaped from jail," he added in a more normal tone of voice.

4

Vledder paced up and down the cluttered, noisy detective room. His facial expression was pinched. It was as if a thundercloud surrounded him. He was so enraged he felt himself choking. None of the other officers had ever seen Vledder loose his temper. He tore his tie from around his neck in one violent gesture. Sputtering, he stopped in front of DeKok's desk.

"How is it possible," he cried furiously.

DeKok shrugged his shoulders.

"He knocked down one of the guards," he said tonelessly. "During the ensuing commotion he managed to escape."

The young inspector leaned over the desk and slapped both hands down in front of DeKok.

"Months' of work," he roared. "All that tedious detail for nothing—one letter at a time for two months and all blown away. Months of work flushed down the toilet. It took that long before we had enough evidence to make an arrest. We had no lives, tracking down every little thing we could think of and for what? A dangerous suspect like him ... at least two murders ... they let him walk away, just like that."

DeKok shook his head.

"No, not just like that. The guard is in the hospital with a fractured jaw."

Vledder fell down in the chair behind his desk.

"But even so, it should never have happened!" He was still angry. "It's getting to be a habit. Everyday one, two, three, or more just take off."

With an angry look Vledder looked at his partner, mentor and friend. At one time he had been assigned to DeKok as an assistant, but now Vledder was a full-fledged inspector in his own right. His rank was substantially the same as DeKok's. But although DeKok would never rise above his present rank, Vledder was slated to rise in the ranks. DeKok never doubted Vledder would one day make Commissaris, maybe even Chief Constable. But in their day-to-day dealings DeKok always, subtly, remained the senior partner and Vledder the junior partner. Neither man was conscious of it. Neither really cared. They were a highly effective team, each partner trusting the other implicitly. DeKok empathized with Vledder's current protestations of "wasted" work. As a junior, he had performed under what seemed to be vows of obedience, poverty, and, yes, chastity. Junior officers of any rank had meager lives outside of work.

"And now what?" queried Vledder. "We have to start the hunt all over again?" He growled some barely audible curses. He knew all about DeKok's aversion to strong language. "And who knows where to find him?" he continued. "Do we know his plans? We can hardly provide protection for all the rich old folks on his list. Besides, he'll probably start a whole new list." Again he slammed his fist on the desk.

DeKok pursed his lips, then pulled out his lower lip, and let it plop back. It was one of his more annoying habits. After almost a minute of this, he looked at Vledder.

"It never entered my mind to warn the people on the list. I'm afraid it would cause them to panic. We will ask Meindert Post to keep a surreptitious eye on the addresses."

"Well, at least it's something," admitted Vledder. "What else do you have in mind?"

"How methodical was Igor?"

"What do you mean?"

"Well, do we know if he followed his list in a particular order ... from beginning to end, or whatever."

Vledder shook his head.

"No, Mrs. Linshot was third in line and Samuel Lion was almost at the bottom of the list. There's no hope there."

DeKok nodded.

"How many people on the list altogether?"

Vledder touched a few keys on his keyboard.

"Twelve," he said.

"So there are ten left."

"Eleven, actually. Mrs. Bildijk wasn't part of the list, but her name and address are in the agenda."

DeKok did not react. He remained seated for a while, staring into the distance. Then he slowly rose out of his chair and waddled over to the peg where he kept his coat. He struggled into the wet garment. Vledder made as if to follow him.

"Where are you going?"

DeKok grinned.

"I'm going to see Lowee. I'm thirsty."

Lowee, usually referred to as Little Lowee because of his small stature, rubbed his small hands on his greasy vest. A happy grin lit up his narrow, ferret-like face.

"Well, well," he chirped jovially. "Da Great Cop done found the way again. Itsa bin days and days."

DeKok hoisted himself onto a barstool.

"I know, I know," he sighed. "It's been too long. But what do you want? Duty before pleasure, you know."

Vledder seated himself next to his partner. He was getting used to this dark, intimate bar where prostitutes gathered between clients and tried to forget the more sordid aspects of the world's oldest profession. Lowee himself was known to be a small-time fence, but had only been caught once, by DeKok. These days he was either more circumspect, or DeKok paid less attention to his nefarious activities. Over the years a real friendship had developed between the small, mousy barkeeper and the rugged old cop. DeKok was the only person in Amsterdam Lowee trusted. And with his intimate knowledge of the underworld he was always a reliable source of information.

Lowee turned philosophical, or maybe he was just being a good bartender. "All duty and no play gonna shorten you life for nuttin." He then produced a venerable bottle of cognac and showed the label.

"Same recipe?" he asked.

DeKok nodded, but did not speak. The question was merely an introduction to a by now almost hallowed tradition. Vledder and DeKok watched in silence as Lowee produced three large snifters and started to pour.

Vledder raised his glass and sniffed appreciatively. Under DeKok's guidance he was rapidly becoming a connoisseur of good cognac. DeKok held his glass up against the light and waited until Lowee, too, had picked up his glass. With silent enjoyment they took the first sip. DeKok closed his eyes and followed the golden liquid as it found its way to his stomach. It was a serious, private meditation.

The slight barkeeper was the first to break the silence.

"Youse look sorta down," he stated.

Lowee spoke a type of Dutch even native Dutchmen found hard to understand. His language was the language of the underworld and the gutter. A mixture of several languages with meanings far removed from their original intent and almost all mispronounced. The closest thing to *Bargoens,* as it is called, would probably be a mixture of Cockney, Yiddish, ungrammatical Dutch, and Papiamento, (a mixture of Dutch, Portuguese, and African dialects).

DeKok was the only cop in the Netherlands who both understood and spoke Bargoens, but he couldn't bring himself to speak it.

DeKok nodded.

"That's an acute observation."

The barkeeper laughed.

"C'mon, DeKok, how badsa gonna be?" He did not wait for an answer. His face became serious. "I done read about it inna fishwrap ... the killer ofda old geezers done fled an' you gottit bad, ain'cha?"

Lowee's actual words were almost incomprehensible, but DeKok understood him. Vledder, too, was getting more and more adept at interpreting Lowee. "Fish wrap" referred to a newspaper. The Dutch eat a lot of fish and the remains are invariably wrapped in an old newspaper before disposal. It was also a reference to the way the British traditionally serve fish and chips, in a newspaper.

DeKok nodded and rubbed the back of his neck.

"Yes, Lowee," he admitted. "I'm worried about it. He's a strange man, irresponsible, unpredictable, and vicious. He's capable of anything."

Little Lowee shook his head in disapproval. "The hoosegow these days is justa movie house widda conti ... contin ... widda ongoing pergamme. They's goin' in an out asday like. I got some come in here and I knows they's suppose to be in jail."

"But you serve them?"

Lowee looked flabbergasted.

"Yessir," he said, irritation in his voice. "Wadda ya want? Itsa ma biznez youse unnerstand."

DeKok could not help but smile at the reaction. He pointed at the empty glasses.

"Pour one more for the road," he suggested.

The small barkeeper obeyed with the alacrity of the good publican.

For a long time they remained silent, enjoying the cognac. At the end of the bar a woman in a hoarse voice wailed the blues. Some of the other people at the various tables sang along. When the last word finally died away, everybody applauded vigorously. A few people stood up and placed some money in a jar for the singer. No one gave coins, just paper money.

Little Lowee looked on from behind the bar.

"Ol' Kate," he said almost tenderly. "She can't make it onner back nomore."

Young Vledder looked at his watch and yawned. His day had started early and the cognac made him sleepy. He put his glass down.

"If you hear something, Lowee, let us know."

Lowee looked scandalized. Maybe Vledder was tired. But as sleepy as he might be, he certainly was not in a position to make any requests. He was here with DeKok and there was a protocol, even among trusted friends.

DeKok looked up from his glass.

"Yes, Lowee, let me know what you hear."

The scandalized look disappeared from Lowee's face and was replaced by a look of understanding.

"For sure, DeKok, iffen I hears somewhat of Igor, I'll give youse da high sign."

DeKok seemed to freeze in position. Suddenly he looked sharply at the small barkeeper. "You said *Igor*. As far as I know that was not in the papers, Lowee. And we haven't mentioned his name to you."

Lowee grinned sheepishly.

"Among da penoze (underworld), Igor Stablinsky ain't exactum no stranger, youse know."

"You know him?"

"He's done bin here one time, or so. Had somewhat goin' wid onofda gals ... young chicky. She usta work da Leiden Street. I think she got Big H now." He paused, looked at Vledder and explained: "She's a heroine addict," he added precisely.

DeKok leaned forward.

"Any idea how I can find the girl?"

Little Lowee glanced quickly around the bar to assure himself no one could listen in on the conversation. He was not known as a "snitch" and was not about to loose that reputation. It would be bad for business, not to mention his health. He talked to DeKok freely, because he trusted the old sleuth. As far as he knew only DeKok, Vledder, and Lowee himself knew he sometimes fed information to DeKok. So far as Lowee was concerned, that was already three people too many. Friendship has its obligations, so he helped DeKok whenever he could. Still he hesitated. Igor was not someone to underestimate.

"Why don't you," he said, suddenly in very precise Dutch, "visit number two seventeen, Long Leiden Side Street, third floor in the back."

"Who lives there?"

"Crazy Chris. He gotta social conscience. One stop for heroine, crack, and condoms—safe sex, youse know," he cackled.

"Crazy Chris," repeated DeKok.

"Yep," confirmed Lowee, "he tells you of Igor's girlfriend, alright."

From rear Fort Canal they passed through Old Acquaintance Alley in the direction of Old Church Square. Now they were on home turf. It was busy in the Quarter, as usual. It was already dark outside. Soon the Red Light District would be in full swing and the pace of the police station would heat up, as well. The old, renowned, Warmoes Street Police Station was DeKok's alma mater. Some referred to it as the Dutch "Hill Street." Among police officers it was known as the busiest police station in Europe. Situated on the edge of Amsterdam's Red Light District, it was hemmed in by the harbor. The polyglot population encompassed all strata of society, from aristocrats to day laborers, from drug dealers to respectable business people. A hundred or more languages could be heard in the Quarter. Churches were virtual bedfellows with brothels, so to speak. Here, the bars never closed; someone was always willing to pay for the refuge, meager though it might be.

Vledder and DeKok absorbed the atmosphere while they worked their way through crowds gathering in front of windows backlit in shades of pink and red. The prostitutes were beginning to display themselves for the evening trade.

"Ask for Igor's girlfriend," said Vledder. He looked at DeKok. "Have you heard yet about a so-called girlfriend?"

DeKok shook his head and made a dismissive gesture.

"Perhaps she plays only a minor role in his life. We have not been able to uncover a hint of her existence.

Vledder looked at the tower clock of Old Church.

"You want to follow up tonight, still?"

DeKok nodded emphatically.

"After he fled, Igor didn't have many choices. Our boy is a classic sociopath, not to say a psychopath. He has almost no friends, but he's smart enough to expect us to watch his known associates. His own house is impossible as a hiding place. That's a given. If he remained in town, it's just possible he's with the girlfriend."

Vledder yawned again. Fighting the need to sleep was making him irritable.

"Young heroin whores almost never have regular addresses," he objected. "More than likely, this one is holed up in some abandoned building or she's renting a crib by the hour in some flea bag hotel. He sighed. "We could have more fun searching through haystacks (or free clinics) for needles."

DeKok looked at his partner and friend, gauging his condition with a practiced eye.

"Come we'll keep walking," he said. "It will clear out the cobwebs."

Vledder followed reluctantly.

Long Leiden Side Street was narrow and dark. Near the end, on the side of Mirror Canal, the lights had all but vanished. Only a few of the remaining lights were still operating. Dark shapes flitted by as they looked up at number two hundred and seventeen. It was a sad section of street. It was too narrow for a trash truck and the inhabitants had apparently never bothered to take their refuse to the end of the street for collection.

The door to number two hundred and seventeen was damaged. The paint was peeling and there was a crack in the upper panel. Around the lock were signs of forced entry. A greasy piece of rope protruded from the letter slot in the door. Vledder and DeKok both knew the arrangement. Anyone wanting to open the door pulled on the rope, which was connected to a latch. Once the latch popped, the door easily opened. It was the usual way to access Dutch homes in multi-story buildings. It was common for one family to occupy a single floor. The families shared a common staircase and corridor. The rooms on each floor came out on the corridor, since each house was originally meant as a single-family dwelling. The latch arrangement was invented to allow children of working parents to enter when they came home from school.

DeKok pulled on the rope and pushed against the door. As he had expected, the door opened easily. Followed by Vledder he hoisted his two hundred pounds up the narrow, creaking staircase. Vledder provided illumination from a flashlight. On the third floor they saw light streaming from under a door in the back. DeKok approached the door and opened it slowly.

A man was seated on a small sofa in the dingy room. A black sweater and black jeans clung to his fat like the casing on a sausage. The effect was not minimizing. He rose and walked toward his visitors.

"What do you want?" he asked, unsmiling.

DeKok smiled.

"My name is DeKok," he said with a winning smile. "DeKok with kay-oh-kay." He pointed a thumb at Vledder. "And this …"

He was interrupted by the man's attempt to turn around

and go back into the room. DeKok reached out and seemingly without effort pulled the man closer.

"Don't worry about your nasty business. That's not why
we're here."

He pushed and forced the man to sit back on the sofa.

"We just want some information," he added.

"Information?"

"You're Chris, aren't you. Better known as Crazy
Chris?"

The man grunted.

"I don't like surprises. People don't just come here unan-
nounced. What in hell do you want from me?"

DeKok did not answer at once, but held the man's eyes
with his own.

"I take it you've figured out who we are?"

The man snorted.

"If I hadn't known your names, I would have figured it
out from your bad suits ... you're cops."

"That's right," said DeKok cheerfully. "We're inspectors
from Warmoes Street Station." His tone became more serious. "We're here to ask about Igor Stablinsky's girlfriend."

Crazy Chris suddenly looked scared.

"Igor's old lady?"

"Yes."

"German Inge, did you find her?"

Vledder and DeKok glanced at each other. Then DeKok
studied Crazy Chris for a moment.

"What did you mean did we find her?"

The heavy man waved his arms around.

"News doesn't travel so fast, after all. German Inge has
been missing for at least two weeks."

"Missing?"

Crazy Chris nodded with emphasis.

"Murdered, most likely."

They were dejected as they made their way back to the station house. The rain kept coming down harder. DeKok pulled up the collar of his coat and pulled his hat deeper over his eyes. He glanced at Vledder.

"Had you heard anything about a missing girl?"

"Yes," nodded Vledder. "There was a report about a missing Ingeborg Seidel from Hanover. Nineteen years old. She was last seen getting into a car on Leiden Square."

"Tag number?"

Vledder shook his head.

"None, and no description. We got zip, not even model and make of the car. There was some vague information about a cream colored car." He shrugged his shoulders. "But in the dark it could have been anything from beige to canary yellow."

DeKok groaned. But he did not question the information. Vledder read all reports and remembered most of them.

"The poor girl, who knows what happened to her. Not to mention it doesn't bode well for our efforts to track down Igor Stablinsky before the day is done."

They proceeded in silence. The rain was now coming down in sheets and DeKok licked the drops that came down his nose and looked at the neon lights mirrored in the wet pavement.

Vledder finally broke the silence.

"You think that Igor has something to do with Inge's disappearance?"

DeKok shook his head.

"It's hard to say. I suspect that if German Inge is indeed dead, it may have been an occupational hazard."

"You don't really believe one of her customers killed her?"

"Yes, I'm afraid it's quite likely. The life makes these women especially vulnerable. Few, if any, carry weapons. When one of them steps into a stranger's car, she's no better off than a child, regardless her age or experience. A prostitute relies on instinct and the word on the street to avoid predatory monsters. In fact, she is the lowest link in a complex food chain."

Vledder nodded agreement.

They had now reached Damrak, the wide shopping street that lead to the dam and ran almost parallel to Warmoes Street, generally believed to be the oldest street in Amsterdam. There was no question about the fact that Warmoes Street Station was the oldest police station in the city.

As they entered the station, Sergeant Kusters, the current watch commander, motioned toward DeKok.

"Just about fifteen minutes ago, I had a woman on the phone. She was beside herself and kept asking for you."

"You have a name?"

Kusters checked his notes.

"Oh, yes, of course. The name was Bildijk, Isolde Bildijk. She kept going on about geese."

DeKok waited for more information.

"What else," he prompted finally.

"Her geese are all dead," said Kusters.

5

Commissaris Buitendam, the tall, stately Chief of Warmoes Street Station gestured with an elegant hand toward the chair in front of his desk.

"Sit down, DeKok," he said in his usual, affected voice. "I need to consult with you."

Reluctantly, DeKok took a seat. He was always suspicious when the commissaris invited him to his office. He certainly didn't dislike his chief. As long as the commissaris left him alone to do his work, DeKok was perfectly content. Under those circumstances the relationship could even be described as cordial. Conflict didn't arise until the commissaris (heavily influenced by the judge advocate) corrected DeKok for some behavior or other. Then he became obstreperous, even illogical. He cherished the freedom to handle his cases according to his own ideas and methods. Any infringement on that he considered as an invasion of his privacy and an insult to both his person and his professionalism.

"What about?" asked DeKok.

Commissaris Buitendam gave his subordinate a winning smile.

"We need to talk about geese."

"What kind of geese"

"Mrs. Bildijk's geese."

DeKok half closed his eyes and leaned his head to one side.

"Just so I understand … this is about some geese?"

"They are dead."

DeKok grinned.

"I know that. Kusters told me late last night."

The commissaris did not react. He shuffled some papers on his desk and separated a report. Then he looked up.

"The geese were poisoned."

DeKok shrugged his shoulders disinterestedly.

"No doubt," he said resignedly. "They could hardly all have died at once of natural causes." He grimaced. "It would be highly unusual to run across a gaggle or two of carcasses."

The commissaris was not amused.

"I want you," Buitendam said in an official voice, "to investigate the death of those geese."

DeKok could not believe his ears. He stared at his chief, incredulous.

"Me?" he exclaimed finally. "You want *me* to investigate? I have nothing to do with those geese nor do I wish to have anything to do with them. Mrs. Bildijk lives along the Amstel, in the Twenty-third Precinct. Let them handle it."

Buitendam held up a hand as if to stem the flow of words.

"Didn't you investigate these geese only yesterday?"

DeKok shook his head.

"I've no interest in those geese, or any other geese," he said in a bantering tone of voice. "Anybody with enough space can keep geese as far as I'm concerned. Personally … I wouldn't. I don't particularly like geese. I think they're nasty animals. I woul—"

Again the commissaris stemmed the flow of words. This time he slapped the top of his desk with a flat hand.

"Let's end the discussion, DeKok," he said sharply. "You and Vledder visited Mrs. Bildijk yesterday in connection with those geese."

DeKok sighed elaborately.

"I went there," he said patiently, "because Mrs. Bildijk's name was written down in Igor Stablinsky's agenda. There was no other reason." He spread wide his arms. "The lady has a sort of love-hate relationship with her gardener. I'm afraid her geese have become the victims of a grudge match."

Commissaris Buitendam rose from his chair and pointed a finger at DeKok.

"I want you to investigate this matter."

DeKok grinned without mirth and without respect.

"Geese ... dead geese." he snorted. "It's a mockery ... what a ridiculous waste, looking into the demise of some eccentric's attack birds."

The chief pressed his lips together. He took a deep breath.

"You heard what I said," Buitendam said with a distant voice, as if the conversation had already been concluded. "The decision stands," he added.

Slowly DeKok came to his feet. He leaned toward the commissaris. His friendly boxer face was expressionless.

"Igor Stablinsky has escaped," hissed DeKok. "Did you know that, or don't you read reports unless prompted by influential people."

Beginning at his neckline, the chief turned pink and then distinctly red. A tic developed along his jaw line. He pointed an outstretched arm at the door.

"OUT!"

DeKok left.

"Well, how did it go?"

DeKok made a helpless gesture. "That went well," he said under his breath.

"The commissaris became angry ... again and sent me from the room."

Vledder shook his head in disapproval.

"You're going too far. You drive the man to the brink ... at this rate he'll soon be ready for the men in the white coats." He smiled. "What did you fight about this time?"

DeKok waved vaguely in the direction of the office he had just left.

"The commissaris, in his infinite wisdom, wishes me to investigate the death of the widow's blighted geese."

Vledder sank back in his chair, mouth agape.

"But ... but that's none of our business. It's a case for the Twenty-third. Besides, it isn't exactly homicide, now, is it?"

DeKok nodded.

"That's what I tried to tell the commissaris. I couldn't care less about those pests. It is critical to locate Igor Stablinsky. As long as that psychopath is on the loose, there's always the danger he'll find more prey." He paused and sighed. "The commissaris is of a different opinion." He uttered a short, derisive laugh. "Dead geese!" There was a world of exasperation in the last two words.

Vledder moved to a chair in front of DeKok's desk. He straddled the chair and rested his arms across the back. He lowered his head and rested it on his folded arms and looked at DeKok. Then he shook his head.

"I just can't understand the chief's motives."

DeKok lifted the Stablinsky file from his desk drawer and placed it on top of the desk.

"Oh," he said, "that's easy. I'm certain that the rich Mrs. Bildijk has a number of influential acquaintances. Some "friends," via the judge advocate, have put pressure on the commissaris."

Vledder snorted.

"In that case, what's *her* motive?"

"Protection."

Vledder could no longer remain seated. He stood up and towered over DeKok.

"She can afford a protective service ... a bodyguard. She can hardly expect public servants to—"

DeKok's look interrupted the beginning tirade.

"It must be terrifying," said DeKok, "to have such a deadly fear of some unknown, unidentified danger while you're confined to a wheelchair. You understand ... without help she can never escape that fear ... that feeling of doom. I think that's what Mrs. Bildijk really wants from us, is to remove the source of her fear."

"And if there's no such source?"

DeKok seemed to consider the question for a moment.

"Then ... then she might very well be ready ... how did you put that ... ready for the men in white coats."

There was a knock on the door to the detective room. One of the detectives nearer the door yelled something and the door opened. A medium tall, slightly corpulent man entered and spoke a few words to the detective near the door. The detective pointed and the man slowly approached DeKok's desk. He halted in front of the desk and made an awkward bow.

"You ... eh, you're Inspector DeKok?"

DeKok nodded.

"With kay-oh-kay ... at your service."

The man smiled briefly.

"My name is Ivo ... Ivo Bildijk. I arrived this morning from Antwerp after an alarming telephone conversation about poisoned geese. I would like to talk with you about my aunt ... Aunt Isolde."

DeKok gave the man a searching look. He estimated his visitor to be in the early thirties. He had a fleshy, reddish face that looked like it had a continuous blush. His flaxen hair stuck to his head with too much hair oil. Under a small, bulbous nose he sported a narrow moustache that drooped around the corners of his mouth. His blue eyes were watery and myopic.

With a polite gesture, DeKok pointed at a chair next to his desk.

"Have a seat," he said. "Why do you suppose I would be interested?"

The remark seemed to confuse the younger man.

"I ... I understood from Aunt Isolde that ... that you are in charge of the case." He seated himself and pulled up his pants legs to preserve the creases. His face was mild with the expression of a concerned relative. "She feels you're the only inspector able enough to stand by her."

"Stand by her for what?"

Ivo seemed surprised at the question.

"But I thought you knew that as well." He was upset as well as confused. "My aunt is being threatened."

"How?"

Ivo Bildijk shrugged his shoulders.

"We don't know that. My brother and sister are as much in the dark as we are."

DeKok looked a question.

"Who are your brother and sister?" he asked after a long pause.

Ivo smiled apologetically.

"Sorry, I mean my brother Izaak and my sister Irmgard. They feel close to this case as well. You see, we're Aunt Isolde's only heirs. We ... eh ... we inherit everything if she ... eh ... if ..." He did not complete the sentence, but made a vague gesture.

DeKok looked at him evenly.

"Is she planning to die?" he asked brutally.

Bildijk seemed stunned.

"How ... how do you mean?"

"Is Aunt Isolde planning to die in the near future?" he asked impatiently.

Ivo Bildijk scratched the back of his ear, obviously embarrassed.

"No ... no," he stammered, "n-no, I ... I don't think so. Of course she isn't. But in the letters it says that she'll be murdered."

"Murdered?

Bildijk nodded vehemently.

"Aunt Isolde has received several letters, all saying she will die soon." He swallowed. "Aunt Isolde takes these letters very much to heart. She grows more and more distressed, and she has holed up in her house. She's terrified. Although she doesn't say so in so many words, I think from her attitude, she suspects one of us."

"You, your brother, or your sister?"

Bildijk waved his hands in a gesture that suggested both puzzlement and ambivalence.

"She feels we're the only ones that can profit by her death."

"And is that so?"

Ivo Bildijk reflected.

"We're not rich, of course," he said carefully. "Aunt Isolde's inheritance would be most welcome to all three of us. One must be realistic, after all. But that's no reason to wish her dead." He paused and placed his hands on his knees. "Besides, Aunt Isolde isn't the only one from whom we inherit. Our Uncle Immanuel is also very well off … he has no children and is older than Aunt Isolde."

"So he may die sooner."

"Indeed."

DeKok pulled his lower lip out and then let it plop back. He repeated the unpleasant activity several times.

"Has your uncle received threatening letters?"

"I don't know," answered Ivo, sighing. "If he has, I haven't heard anything about it. He lives in a villa near Bussum. He lives with an old housekeeper who is also mentioned in the will. We visit a few times per year. Uncle Immanuel has the beginnings of arteriosclerosis and is slightly demented. That can give startling reactions. Sometimes he doesn't even recognize us." A tender smile fled across his face. "I imagine Uncle Immanuel would not even bother to open any threatening letters. He would either throw them away, or put them in a drawer somewhere."

DeKok nodded his understanding.

"You see how relative everything is … unopened threatening letters have no effect."

Ivo studied DeKok's bland face.

"You mean that Aunt Isolde should not have read the threatening letters?"

DeKok smiled.

"Who can control human curiosity?" Then he looked closer at Ivo Bildijk. "But you, too, think Aunt Isolde's letters are the real thing." It was not a question.

The young man shook his head uncertainly.

"I've read them. And I can tell you that the content is truly menacing. I can well understand why Aunt Isolde fears for her life. And now the affair with the poisoned geese ... she could have died from sheer panic."

For several seconds DeKok looked at the younger man. The old sleuth's face had become expressionless.

"Perhaps, Mr. Bildijk, someone intended your aunt to die of fright."

Ivo Bildijk left, announcing that he, a loving nephew, considered it his duty to move in with his aunt for the time being. Vledder moved over and occupied the recently vacated chair. All during the interview he had made copious notes and at the same time had surreptitiously entered certain data in his computer. DeKok was certain a fresh report was nearly ready to emerge from the printer.

"While we were there," said Vledder, "she said her fears were non-specific. Strangely enough, she never mentioned any threatening letters."

"Perhaps she didn't think the timing was right." DeKok paused for a moment in deep thought. "Even so," he continued finally, "those letters must have started to come some time ago. Her fear increased, causing her to order her gardener to destroy his dogs and get the geese. Next she began to pester officers of the Twenty-third constantly. Those are clear indicators she was becoming desperate."

"Then why did she not share the information with us? Now she has a nephew come all the way from Antwerp to tell us that she's been receiving threatening letters."

DeKok nodded in agreement.

"The death of her geese must have shaken her considerably. She will have recognized it as a direct threat to her safety. This morning, after the dead geese were discovered, she clearly decided to launch some sort of counter-offensive. Through whatever relations she has, she put pressure on our own commissaris and sent her nephew to reinforce the demand for action. I think she must feel that her situation is precarious."

Vledder looked surprised.

"Do you really think that she's about to be murdered?"

DeKok did not answer. He stared in the distance, preoccupied. Then he shook his head, as if to clear it. A smile spread around his lips.

"You know, my boy, I'm starting to get interested in those geese."

"The commissaris will be so happy," grinned Vledder.

The old sleuth stood up. He pointed at Vledder's computer.

"Find out all you can about Ivo. We need to know what he does for a living, where he lives in Antwerp, etc. I also would like some information about nephew Izaak and niece Irmgard. Put your little magic box to work and let me know what you find."

Vledder stood up.

"So you think those three are involved?"

DeKok grinned.

"When there's a fortune at stake, a person can get some twisted ideas."

He moved in the direction of his raincoat, as the phone on DeKok's desk started to ring. Vledder leaned over and lifted the receiver. DeKok turned and waited.

After a brief conversation Vledder replaced the receiver.

"Well?" asked DeKok.

"My magic box will have to wait a while. Someone spotted Igor Stablinsky."

"Where?"

"He's driving a stolen BMW through Bussum."

"And Uncle Immanuel lives nearby there."

Vledder nodded.

6

They drove from Damrak to Rokin. A shy sun peeked through a layer of racing clouds, backlighting up the Royal Palace. Then a thick, black cloud obscured the sun and unloaded a new supply of heavy rain. DeKok relished the quickly changing scene. He loved Amsterdam, no matter the weather. Unlike Rome or Paris, Amsterdam did not need sunshine. Amsterdam's beauty was made for soft, rainy days and nights.

He looked aside at Vledder whose capable hands guided the old VW through the heavy traffic on the slick streets. He felt a bond with the younger man. How many perplexing cases had they solved together? He could recall seventeen, maybe more. He often had trouble remembering the details, but he always remembered the first time he had worked with Vledder. Warmoes Street was still under the previous commissaris. Vledder had been instrumental in having DeKok recalled from his vacation to solve the murder of a prostitute. Afterward they became inseparable as a team. Vledder was also the one who had started to name their cases. DeKok smiled as he thought of some of the names. There was the case of 'The Somber Nude.' DeKok still experienced a pang of regret when he remembered the beautiful Kristel. The cases started to run together in his mind— 'The Dead Harlequin,' 'The Romantic Murder,' 'The Dancing Death.'

Vledder would probably label the current case something like 'The Deadly Geese,' or 'The Geese of Death.' He smiled and pushed the memories to the back of his mind.

"Do you know where the car originated?"

"The BMW?"

"Whatever, the car Igor was driving."

It was Vledder's turn to smile. DeKok looked on identifying car make, model, and year like any other trivia; he did not think of cars in those terms. He identified cars by colors. If they were big, he thought they were probably American. If they were square, DeKok would label them Rolls Royces. Other than that he identified them as small, fast, dirty, or whatever.

"Yes, the car was stolen in Amsterdam. It disappeared from Amstel Road within hours after he escaped from jail. Looks as though he kept on using the same car."

"Still?"

"No, cops discovered the car in Amersfoort early this morning. It was parked between other cars near Our Dear Lady Church. The right front fender was slightly damaged, probably in a recent accident."

"Is anything known about that?"

"No ... they're investigating."

"How did they spot Igor in Bussum?"

Vledder smiled.

"The Bussum police were doing routine safety inspections. You know how that goes; they pull over a car at random and make sure it's mechanically sound. You'd be amazed how many people drive around in cars that shouldn't be on the road. For instance ..."

DeKok interrupted him.

"I don't care about that, tell me about Igor."

"Well, as I said, the Bussum police were performing

safety inspections. One of the cars they waved to the side was this red BMW. At first he slowed down, as if to pull over, but then he floored it and took off. One of the cops got a good enough look to recognize the driver as Igor Stablinsky. As you know, I sent his picture out on an APB."

"Then what?"

"They immediately amended my original APB with the information about the car and gave an extra heads-up to all posts in and around Bussum."

"Why did they not pursue?"

"No time. They had one van and a single cruiser. The cruiser was behind the van and all the cops were outside the vehicles, directing traffic, or performing inspections. The BMW disappeared onto a side road before they could even begin to pursue him. They did the next best thing; one got to the radio immediately and amended the APB, as I told you."

DeKok grunted.

"Meanwhile, Igor has had plenty of time to ditch the car. By now he's long gone—in a freshly stolen car."

"Sounds about right," Vledder answered.

"What about Uncle Immanuel? Did you tell the Bussum police about Igor's interest in rich old men?"

Vledder did not answer at once. He shifted down to skillfully avoid a group of bicycles. For a few moments all his attention was taken by the traffic.

"Yes," he said then. "I brought them up to speed and they promised to stay alert."

They proceeded in silence. Suddenly DeKok sat up straight.

"But Uncle Immanuel was not mentioned in Igor's agenda, was he?"

Vledder looked startled.

"You're right. I don't think so. I'll check just to be sure, but I don't think so. Maybe we're subconsciously combining the two cases, I mean, the geese and Igor. It must be just a coincidence—Igor running into a safety patrol in Bussum. It could have happened anywhere."

"Maybe." DeKok did not sound convinced. Vledder was not sure which part of his argument his partner doubted.

"How do you mean?" prompted Vledder.

"He was seen in Bussum. The car ended up in Amersfoort. He may still be in that general area. Amersfoort and Bussum are not that far apart."

Vledder shrugged.

"So what. That whole area sort of hangs together. Bussum, Naarden, Hilversum, Amersfoort. It's the eastern corner of the province. Other than that I don't see any significance. Do you have any contact addresses in that area?"

DeKok did not answer. He stared out the windshield and seemed lost in thought. It lasted a while. Then he suddenly turned toward Vledder.

"Don't you find it strange that all names in this case start with the letter 'I'?"

The young inspector thought for a moment.

"Yes, you're right … Isolde, Ivo, Izaak, Irmgard, Immanuel … all Bildijks."

"You forgot one."

"Who?"

"Igor … Igor Stablinsky."

DeKok stopped in front of the wrought-iron gates of Happy Lake and looked up at the sign. The gilded letters against the darkening sky somehow seemed eerie, even macabre.

The heavy iron gates hanging from the stone pillars made him think of Urk, his birthplace. There was just such a gate leading to the old cemetery in his hometown. The town was now on a hill, once an island in the Zuyder Zee. He still remembered a youthful fascination with the iron gates of the cemetery as a young boy. It had been an imposing portal between two towns, one for the living, one for the dead. One could look through the ironwork; so death was never far away, even as he kept a foothold in the town of the living. Through the gaps in the gate, he envisioned the angel of death slumbering beneath the mosaic of headstones. The idea of death was incomprehensible to a child his age, but he could imagine the persona. When old Jelle, the gravedigger, opened the gates wide, young DeKok never ventured past the symbolic or physical portal. Something held him at bay. He never dared take that final step through the gate. Déjà vu made him hesitate again this time.

Vledder did not understand the delay. He passed his older partner and pushed against the right half of the gate. As before, it was not locked. The screeching hinge announced their arrival. They closed the gate behind them and carefully followed the path. The crunching sound of their footsteps on the fine gravel broke a grim silence.

To the left, on the lawn, there were a number of dead bird carcasses. The dead geese had been dragged to one place and heaped in a pile. The tracks still made indentations in the grass. Unpleasant in life, the dead animals made a sad spectacle.

DeKok bent over a goose that rested a few feet from the heap of dead animals; he examined the carcass carefully. There was nothing visible to indicate how the bird had met its end. There were no signs of violence, no wounds, no twisted neck.

The old gardener came closer on wooden shoes. He used his stick to point at the birds.

"Poisoned."

DeKok straightened up and nodded.

"It looks that way," he agreed.

The man cocked his head.

"I just heaped them up here. I didn't know what you would want to do."

"I want them dissected. I want to know what kind of poison has been used."

The old man grinned an evil smile.

"Strychnine."

DeKok looked at him evenly.

"What would make you say that?"

The man used his stick to point in the direction of the coach house.

"A considerable dose vanished from my supply. Probably mixed in with their feed."

"Is any left?"

"The feed?"

"Yes."

"No, I cleaned out the bowls."

For a long time DeKok stared at the dead birds.

"Who," he asked tersely.

The gardener shrugged his shoulders in a vague gesture.

"Whoever it was didn't leave a calling card."

DeKok turned suddenly and confronted the gardener. From close up he stared directly into the other's eyes through his heavy brows.

"Did you do this, Willem?"

The old man stared back calmly.

"No, not me."

Suddenly his lower lip trembled.

"Geese are not my friends, you know." His tone was sad. "They ruin everything for a gardener." He turned his head into the direction of the big house. "But if she wants it ... you understand ... I'm a slave to her will. I do what I'm told, that's it."

For a long moment DeKok looked pensively at the gardener. Then he turned toward Vledder.

"Please make sure someone removes these carcasses."

Vledder nodded.

"I'll use the phone in the house."

The three of them walked toward the house. The gardener walked between the two cops. He pointed at a row of cars parked in front of the coach house.

"It's just like a reunion," he grunted. "She called the entire family together." He snorted. "Ever since those silly geese died, she's consumed by fear."

"That bad?"

The gardener nodded vehemently.

"Oh, yes, she's been on the phone almost constantly. I've never seen her so close to hysteria."

DeKok gave him a casual glance.

"I heard she received threatening letters."

Willem seemed surprised.

"What? Who told you that?"

"Her nephew, Ivo, made a special trip to the police station to tell us. Apparently Dear Aunt Isolde sent him to deliver the message."

The gardener shook his head.

"So she demands I keep it a secret."

DeKok smiled.

"So, there *are* threatening letters?"

Willem nodded.

"Oh, yes. She's been receiving them for about six months, at least. Somebody's writing her to tell her that she's going to be killed soon."

"Have you read the letters?"

"Not all of them, I think."

"How many?"

The old man raised two fingers.

"Two of them. One morning she called me in, had me sit down and gave me the letters to read. They said she had not much longer to live … they alluded to the hire of a contract killer."

"You didn't take them as crank letters? I mean you felt she should take them seriously?"

"Oh, yes. They scared me, all right."

"What did the letters look like?"

"They were typed, and sent in blue business envelopes. The inside of each envelope was lined. Whenever I get the mail from the box, I look for such an envelope, one without a sender's name. That's how I know she has received another threatening letter."

DeKok nodded to himself.

"How often does this happen?"

"Lately, they come at least once a week."

"Did the sender ask for money … in the letters?"

Willem shook his head.

"I haven't read anything like that. I don't think it's about money … I think someone just wants to scare her."

"Why?"

The gardener shrugged his shoulders.

"No idea," he commented.

"Why didn't she call the police sooner?"

"She's asked for protection all along."

"But she never said anything about the letters?"

Again the old man shook his head.

"No, she didn't. And she wouldn't let anyone else tell the police about them."

"Why not?"

That question seemed to suddenly irritate the gardener. A blush spread over his cheeks. With an annoyed gesture he pointed at the entrance to the mansion.

"Why don't you ask her yourself?"

Everyone gathered in a soberly furnished room. The sole relief was a view of the meadows from a bay window. Mrs. Bildijk held court in the center, stiffly upright in her ornate chair. Her nephew Ivo stood to her right. His plump left hand rested on the back of the chair.

DeKok ambled toward the chair while he studied the faces. There were no physical similarities, no recognizable familial resemblances between the old lady and her nephew. But there was something in the imperious way they looked at him that suggested a common heritage.

To the left was a wide wooden bench with embroidered cushions. He noticed a man and a woman, seated as far apart as was possible on the bench. Three children stood behind the bench, as if on parade, two boys and a girl. DeKok estimated the older boy to be about sixteen. He was a solidly built young man in a blue T-shirt with a capital letter "S" on the chest. He had the look of a sheepdog puppy with tousled blond bangs hiding his eyebrows. The boy next to him was more fragile, almost scrawny. A black sweater, several sizes too large, made an untidy impression. The girl looked to be about ten years old. She wore a red velvet dress with a short embroidered cape, almost like a pelerine. Long blonde hair hung down below her shoulder blades in old-fashioned corkscrew curls. The Bildijk family resemblance was more marked in the faces of the children … each had a sharp nose and high cheekbones.

DeKok stopped in front of the 'throne' and bowed slightly, a hint of a smile on his face.

Mrs. Bildijk nodded condescendingly, gesturing toward her right side.

"Inspector, you already met my nephew, Ivo, this morning. He has reported to me the result of his interview with you." She pointed at the bench with a bony finger. "I'll introduce my nephew Izaak … my niece Irmgard and her three children, Peter, Paul, and Penny. We expect Irmgard's husband this evening. Business affairs prevent him from attending at this time." She looked regally around the room and waved in the direction of Vledder and DeKok. "This is Inspector DeKok and his assistant, Vledder," she said to the room at large.

DeKok shook his head.

"*Colleague* Vledder," he corrected.

Mrs. Bildijk seemed not to have heard him.

"I have summoned both gentlemen," she continued as if there had not been an interruption, "to investigate the death of the geese. This is extremely serious. I took the animals to help protect me … a task the police should have been performing."

She paused for emphasis and looked at DeKok with a disapproving expression.

"Yesterday," she went on, "I already expressed to you my concerns. I had a strong suspicion something would happen to my geese ... something terrible. My suspicion was obviously well founded." She raised her chin defiantly. "If the animals have indeed been killed by strychnine poisoning, I insist you arrest my gardener."

DeKok looked vacant.

"Old Willem?" he asked.

"Yes."

DeKok made a doubting gesture.

"I questioned your gardener less than ten minutes ago. He gave me his word he is not responsible for the death of your geese."

Mrs. Bildijk gave him a pitying smile and then looked annoyed.

"And you believe him?"

DeKok hesitated before answering.

"For a police officer," he said carefully, "it's not so much a matter of belief as it is legal proof."

Mrs. Bildijk was getting upset.

"Willem hated the geese. He could hardly hide his dislike of the animals. He has bought strychnine. A significant amount of his supply has since disappeared."

DeKok gave her a winning smile.

"He told me as much."

"And?"

DeKok shook his head, as if in regret.

"None of it is significant. The coach house is not locked at night. It would not be much of a challenge for anyone able-bodied to scale the fence and enter the coach house."

"You think it was an intruder from outside the house—a stranger?"

"It may not have been a complete stranger. More likely,

I think, someone who has been here before … or stayed the night."

Mrs. Bildijk looked at DeKok with disbelief.

"And a person like that goes straight to a cupboard, to a newly purchased supply of strychnine, and poisons my geese." She gestured, as if at a loss for words. "That is … you have to admit … that is … is ludicrous." She moved in her chair and placed herself tight against the back. "I must repeat my demand. Arrest my gardener!"

DeKok shook his head.

"I will not take Willem into custody." he looked at her sharply, then, continued. "There will be no arrest, unless you have evidence Willem is the author of so much as a single threat."

Mrs. Bildijk' tightened her grip on the armrests of her chair. DeKok saw her knuckles whiten.

"Such evidence can be furnished." She spat out the words. With a wild look in her eyes, she looked at her nephew. "Ivo, get the letters," hissing like one of the demised geese.

Ivo walked over to a roll-top desk in the corner of the room. He turned a key and opened the top. He pulled out a drawer. He returned with a bundle of blue envelopes, bound with a purple ribbon.

Mrs. Bildijk took the bundle from him and gave them to DeKok with a theatrical gesture.

"You will note the postmarks," she said severely. "These letters have all been post-marked at Oldkerk. All were dates when Willem shopped for me."

7

Vledder, sitting behind the wheel of the old VW again, gazed at his partner. There was a look of disbelief on his young face. He slapped the steering wheel with his right hand.

"So, why did you not arrest the gardener?" His voice had a tremor of anger and astonishment. "My God, you had sufficient grounds. Mrs. Bildijk is distraught, and with reason. I just bet she's back on the phone, calling every influential person she knows. Before you know it, you'll have the entire bureaucracy all over us … for neglect of duty."

DeKok did not react. He sank down in the seat with an austere look on his face. Vledder's critique did not touch him. As if the words went in one ear and out the other.

Vledder snorted in disgust and did not let up.

"I found those cancellations very significant. She must have noticed early on the letters were always dated on days Willem was away from the house … in Oldkerk. Whether she believed the dates to be coincidental, or not, she kept track." He remained silent for a few seconds. "And as far as those geese are concerned, I found your supposition of an outsider debatable, to say the least." Vledder shoved his lower lip forward and shook his head. "I cannot say that this afternoon was one of your better moments. I must say I've never seen you so ineffectual."

The younger man concentrated on the traffic. DeKok's

silence annoyed him and made him unsure of himself. He well knew about his friend's unpredictability. It would certainly be useless to second-guess him. He tried again, his tone more friendly this time.

"After all, it cannot be coincidence. I mean the post marks."

DeKok raised himself in the seat somewhat and sighed.

"I don't believe Willem is the guilty party."

Vledder gave a short, mocking laugh.

"You speak with forked tongue, DeKok," he asserted. "In your own words: For a police officer it's not so much a matter of what he believes, but what he can prove legally."

DeKok recognized his own words and it elicited a smile.

"Well," he said after a while, "Sometimes I also rely on my knowledge of people. Old Willem is, as far as I can see, not the person we're looking for ... not the man who's threatening Isolde. On the contrary, I think he's in love with her."

Vledder was speechless for a moment.

"What!" he gasped finally. "In love ... with an invalid?"

DeKok looked at his younger colleague. His face was expressionless.

"So," he asked, "you think that's impossible?"

Vledder parked the rickety police car in a lot about a block away from the police station. DeKok hoisted himself slowly from his cramped position and slammed the door. Leaning on the roof of the car, he looked up to the gabled houses that separated them from Warmoes Street. Through a gap in the houses they could just see the back of the station house.

For a moment it seemed the unadorned back wall bulged with all the lusts, passions, heartaches, and emotions of many decades. The dismal flood of feelings began to envelope him, threatening to suffocate him. He waited for the feeling to pass and looked at the lighted window of his chief's office. He knew the commissaris was waiting for him.

He rubbed his chin with his right hand, grinning to himself. He waited for Vledder to lock the doors. They walked through the alley to Warmoes Street side by side. They entered the station house and passed the counter behind which the watch commander presided. It was Meindert Post again.

"There's a guy waiting for you upstairs," he roared in his usual stentorian voice. "He says his name is Crazy Chris. He's got information about some dame you're interested in."

Vledder and DeKok halted and DeKok looked back inquiringly.

"I told him," continued Post, still at the top of his voice, "to give me the message, but he wants to talk only to you two."

Slowly he lumbered toward them from behind the counter.

"But first, I'd talk to the commissaris," he added, almost at a normal volume. "He just came in a while ago. He had the judge advocate with him, Mr. Schaap. They were obviously in a bad mood." He nodded at DeKok. "I am to tell you to report immediately, the moment I see you or you contact us. Sorry, I'm just the messenger."

DeKok waved jovially, hiding his inner qualms. He was afraid he would have to fight off unwanted interference again.

Together with Vledder he climbed the stairs.

"Why don't you find out what Crazy Chris wants to share with us and I'll go see the commissaris."

Vledder gave him a warning look.

"Keep calm," he advised. "Don't loose your temper."

"Why should I?"

"I know you, old friend and … Buitendam isn't all *that* bad."

DeKok knocked on the door and waited patiently for a reaction. He entered diffidently. Then he bowed his head slightly. He consciously assumed that posture. He did not feel up to a confrontation. He firmly resolved not to let any criticism affect him. He would agree to whatever they wanted.

Commissaris Buitendam looked drawn and somehow smaller behind his enormous desk. With an elegant hand he waved to the chair next to him where a dapper little man was seated.

"I am certain no introduction is necessary," he began in his cultured voice, "to Mr. Schaap, our esteemed judge advocate. You two know each other from previous occasions." He coughed discreetly to make an impression. "The reason we're gathered here this evening is a distressing report given to both myself and Mr. Schaap. It concerns your behavior at the house of Mrs. Bildijk. Mrs. Bildijk reports you refused to arrest her gardener, despite the fact there were sufficient legal grounds to do so." He fell silent and pointed an accusing finger at DeKok.

"If so, it is a serious omission, DeKok," the commissaris continued. "Now you and *we* must answer a charge of neglect of duty. Mrs. Bildijk has very influential contacts with the police and in the Department of the Interior, to which we all report." He cleared his throat repeatedly. "Her contacts, these ... ahem, relations have strongly suggested I administer disciplinary punishment for your dereliction of duty."

DeKok bowed his head deeper.

"Well, if it will pacify those ... eh, relations, go ahead and punish me."

Commissaris Buitendam lowered his arm and his accusing finger. The answer took him by surprise. He had braced himself for an argument. He coughed again, this time to hide his uncertainty.

"You will understand, DeKok, I am not empowered to punish you myself. The matter must be referred to a duly organized committee. Nor would it be appropriate for me to simply recommend disciplinary action to that committee. Not with your record."

DeKok shrugged his shoulder.

"You spoke of punishment," he said evenly, his temper in an iron grip. "Well, let it be. What has my record to do with it? If you think I have neglected my duty, you know what you have to do. What else is there to discuss?"

Buitendam gave him a searching look. He did not trust either DeKok's meek behavior, or his tone of voice. He looked at the judge advocate, as if asking for help.

"The judge advocate shares my opinion that the arrest of the gardener was fully justified, given the circumstances it was mandatory."

DeKok suppressed a grin. The concept 'blather' suggested itself strongly. With a supreme effort he suppressed the urge to say it out loud. He gestured vaguely, helplessly.

"I have not arrested Mrs. Bildijk's gardener."

Mr. Schaap interjected a deriding laugh.

"We couldn't help noticing," he said.

DeKok ignored the interruption.

"I have not arrested Mrs. Bildijk's gardener," repeated DeKok, "because I believe him to be innocent. Regardless of any perception to the contrary, police do not care to waste time, effort, and public funds arresting innocent people."

Mr. Schaap shook his head.

"He was and is not innocent."

DeKok gestured feebly.

"All else aside my conscience would not permit me to rob that man of his freedom."

It was too much for the commissaris. He shoved his chair back and stood up.

"Since when," he demanded angrily, "does it depend on your conscience whether or not an arrest takes place?"

DeKok looked defenseless

"Ever since I have been an inspector. And that has been a long time."

The commissaris was clearly losing his temper. Red spots appeared on his cheeks.

"I don't give a ... a ... a crap for your conscience," he roared, beside himself.

DeKok looked at him serenely.

"Nonetheless I do," he said. He nodded to himself as if to confirm his statement. "I do," he repeated. Then he sighed deeply and controlled his breathing as he positively banished any emotions.

"If both of you have decided," DeKok continued after he had gathered himself, "the gardener is guilty, either one of you has plenty of authority to go to Happy Lake and make the arrest himself. Or you could go together."

Buitendam seemed close to exploding.

"You do not decide what we will do," he screamed.

DeKok pressed his lips together and took a deep breath.

"And I," he said finally, "do not make it a policy to compromise my conscience."

Commissaris Buitendam came from behind his desk. For a moment it looked as if he would physically attack DeKok. Then he stopped. He was red, nearly purple, down to his neck. A little vein stood out on his forehead, and his eyes began to bulge dangerously. He pointed at the door with an outstretched arm.

It was a gesture with which DeKok was very familiar. He turned to leave the room. Just as the furious commissaris could open his mouth, Vledder bolted into the office. He stopped in the middle of the room.

"The gardener," he panted.

DeKok looked at him apprehensively.

"What about the gardener?"

Vledder swallowed.

"He's been murdered … apparently, in the coach house."

8

DeKok scowled at both men next to the desk. One was behind it and the other on the side, as if ready to pounce. Slowly they moved toward each other as if seeking mutual support. They looked at each other, still processing their shock. There was nothing left of Buitendam's dignified, aristocratic posture. Mr. Schaap was no longer dapper; he simply looked small and a bit disheveled.

DeKok took a step in their direction. There was a stinging remark on his tongue, but he thought better of it at the last moment. He turned abruptly and followed Vledder out of the room.

Vledder ran down the corridor to the stairs and DeKok followed. DeKok at speed was usually a comic sight. But there was nothing comic about the grim determination on his face.

Vledder guided the decrepit police car through the inner city in the direction of Oldkerk. He entered the narrow tunnel under Weesp Street too fast. Halfway around the bend he suddenly hit the brakes. DeKok banged his head against the side of the car. He shot Vledder a disgusted look.

"Think of my old age. I'd like to enjoy my pension," he said, annoyed. "I haven't that long to go." He gesticulated.

"Why would you be driving like a maniac to get to a murder scene? Dead is dead. I have some experience in these matters. Never have I seen a man or woman come back to life because the police arrived a few minutes sooner."

Vledder again braked hard because a traffic light jumped to red. He held out a protective arm in front of DeKok.

"Sorry," he apologized. "I don't want you to bang your head again." As the light turned green, he added: "I just did not anticipate that."

"The bend in that tunnel has been there since it was built," growled DeKok, only slightly mollified.

Vledder shook his head.

"I mean Willem's death. I don't understand it. What's the sense in murdering an old man like that?"

"Who said anything about murder?"

"Ivo Bildijk called. Ivo was clearly upset and stumbled over his own words. His aunt had pressured him into going to the coach house to talk some sense into the old man. She undoubtedly wanted Ivo to find out whether Willem authored the letters."

"And that's when he found him?"

Vledder nodded.

"His head was bashed in." The young man sighed. "I told Ivo not to touch anything. I also told him to wake the family and have them assemble in the 'throne room' for interrogation."

DeKok frowned.

"They were already in bed?" He seemed surprised.

"Yes, that's what I understood from Ivo, incoherent as he was. This was after the arrival of his brother-in-law, Miller."

DeKok gingerly felt for the growing bulge on his head.

"Miller?" he interrupted.

"Yes, Irmgard's husband, the father of the children."

"The businessman?"

"Exactly. After his arrival they had a light dinner and then they went to bed. Mrs. Bildijk could not fall asleep, however. She called Ivo to talk about the case."

DeKok nodded his understanding.

"And that conversation led Ivo to go to the coach house."

"That's about it. Of course, I couldn't ask him everything in our short phone conversation. Besides, he was much too overwrought. Not to mention Crazy Chris was sitting at my desk, drinking in every word. I had to keep it low key." He shrugged his shoulders. "But there was no way to prevent him from hearing more than he needs to know."

DeKok smiled.

"Crazy Chris. I'd almost forgotten about him. Did he have anything useful?"

Vledder took his notebook out of his pocket and waved it around.

"I've made some notes. It seems that, despite rumors to the contrary, German Inge is still very much alive. She sent some post cards from Hanover to girls who still walk her old beat in Leiden Street."

"No red herrings ... forgeries?"

Vledder put the notebook back in his pocket.

"The cards?"

DeKok nodded emphatically.

"I was onto a burglar some years ago. He had a friend send me a postcard with his signature from the south of Italy. The plan was to provide him an alibi, or just to distract my attention. I caught the burglar committing a robbery the same day the postcard arrived." DeKok grinned. "Who knew I would happen to walk my dog that evening—right in the area where he was committing the theft?"

Vledder shrugged and spread both hands.

"Of course, I haven't seen the cards myself. Crazy Chris claims the girls got the cards from Hanover a few days ago. They recognized Inge's script."

DeKok looked disapproving.

"Please don't do that again!'

"What?"

"Take your hands off the wheel while you're driving."

Vledder remained silent.

DeKok made a soothing gesture.

"She's from Hanover, isn't she?"

The young inspector nodded agreement.

"Born and bred. Perhaps it all became too much for her in the Quarter. Maybe she had an epiphany and decided to return home."

DeKok pursed his lips.

"Maybe, but for how long? Addicts, especially those in the life, usually fall back in their old habits pretty soon. When they ..." He did not complete the sentence. "Regarding the present case ... have you kept the Twenty-third informed?"

"No, not about the latest developments. I guess we'll have to ask them to supply a *herd.*"

Vledder referred to the team of experts, crime scene specialists and high-ranking officers that normally gather info at the scene of a murder, a herd. DeKok usually referred to them as the *Thundering Herd,* after the big band. It was not an endorsement of their subtlety.

DeKok nodded thoughtfully. Vledder busied himself with the radio. After he had passed the information to the Twenty-third Precinct, he switched off the radio. DeKok did not like all those modern conveniences and refused to be contacted by a voice through a contraption. He longed for the time when police officers patrolled on foot, or on a bicycle, and the only contact with the station was through call boxes.

"By the way," said Vledder suddenly. "There's another bit of news."

"Well?"

"A cop caught up with Igor Stablinsky around eight o'clock tonight in the neighborhood of Leiden Square. He was asking after Inge."

"And?"

"According to Crazy Chris, 'les girls' gave him the run-a-round. They did not tell him about the post cards."

"Why not?"

Vledder grinned.

"The other whores are afraid of him. They're avoiding him like HIV. Word is Inge left to get away from him."

The stack of dead geese was still on the lawn. Even in the pale moonlight the limp necks and the dead, staring eyes made for a macabre spectacle. The cumulative odor of death was becoming worse and oppressive. DeKok looked a question at Vledder, who made an apologetic gesture.

"I *did* call," he defended himself. "They promised to collect the bodies today. I'll call again and find out why they haven't done their part."

They passed the dead geese and proceeded along the gravel path. All the windows in the large mansion were lit up. There also was a light on in the upper floor of the coach house. The silhouette of an overweight man slipped past a window.

Vledder walked in the direction of the main building, but DeKok restrained him by pulling on a sleeve.

"Where are you going?"

"To see Mrs. Bildijk. To announce our arrival, what else?"

DeKok shook his head and pointed at the coach house.

"It's an old tradition," he lectured, "for an inspector to have the first look at the victim. Politeness can wait."

Murmuring to himself, Vledder followed his older colleague.

Behind the parked cars, the lower doors of the coach house were opened wide. A big black rat scurried away from them and disappeared somewhere inside.

DeKok almost soundlessly climbed the stairs to the living area. Vledder followed.

Upstairs a door was ajar. A narrow beam of light fell across the landing. Carefully and without sound DeKok approached the door. He opened the door a little wider and looked inside. The first thing to confront him was a man kneeling in front of an old armoire. A drawer partially hung out of the bottom rank. DeKok banged a fist on the upper panel of the door and entered noisily. The man in front of the armoire was startled and tumbled on his back.

DeKok approached and looked down at him.

"Mr. Ivo," DeKok said mockingly, "why are you here?"

The man gathered himself and stood up hastily. He straightened his jacket. There was a blush of shame on his face.

"What do you expect to find in here?" repeated DeKok.

Ivo Bildijk swallowed.

"Nothing ... eh, nothing at all."

DeKok grinned maliciously.

"You kneel in front of an armoire, pull out drawers, but you're looking for nothing?" The skepticism dripped from every word. "Please allow me to observe this is a completely unsatisfactory response."

Bildijk nodded quickly.

"Yes ... eh, yes, I can understand that."

"In that case, may I have an answer more in keeping with the situation in which I found you?" DeKok looked disgusted. "Or is it your habit to peek in the cupboards and drawers of deceased persons?"

Ivo Bildijk shook his head.

"No ... eh, no. Certainly not."

DeKok spread his hands.

"In that case, I repeat, what were you expecting to find?"

Bildijk flicked his tongue along dry lips.

"I ... eh, I hoped to find something that could give me proof that my aunt's gardener indeed wrote the threatening letters."

"And?"

The man gestured helplessly.

"There's nothing."

DeKok came closer. He looked menacing. With one hand he gripped Bildijk's silken necktie. Ivo squirmed under DeKok's angry stare.

"Weren't you told not to touch anything? To leave everything untouched?"

Bildijk nodded.

"Yes, ... eh, that's been ... I've been told, but ..."

"But what?"

Ivo swallowed again. He was now sweating and big drops of perspiration and brilliantine rolled off his forehead.

"Aunt ordered me to look, you understand, before you could get here."

DeKok sighed deeply. He had trouble hiding his disgust. He pointed at the door.

"Get outside," he ordered. "Go to the gate and make sure you receive the people from the technical services, the paramedics and the coroner. Point them in the right direction. Meanwhile, stay away from here unless you're called."

Ivo Bildijk left like a dog with its tail between its legs. DeKok shook his head as he watched him leave. Then he turned.

The old gardener was slumped sideways in his rattan chair, close to his pot-bellied stove. A dark rivulet of venous blood ran down the left side of his head and dripped into a growing pool on the floor. The eyes of the deceased were wide open, big and startled. He had not comprehended what was happening. Gently DeKok closed the man's eyes with his thumb and forefinger. It was a devout, almost loving, gesture.

Then DeKok leaned closer to the body. There was a gaping hole in his gray hair, just above his left ear. The inspector stepped back and took a wider view. He looked for discrepancies in the shrill harmonics of the violent death. It all seemed discouragingly straightforward. The old man had been resting quietly in his chair, when his attacker swiftly struck from behind. Willem died instantaneously from massive blunt instrument trauma.

Suddenly DeKok noticed a short pipe, full of tobacco, on the floor. It had slipped from the hanging, powerless hand. The scene touched him deeply. He promised himself that he would find the killer.

"By God," he said aloud.

9

Vledder glanced aside.

"Did you swear?" he asked incredulously. DeKok never used strong language and was known to disapprove of the use in his hearing.

DeKok shook his head.

"I was talking to Our Dear Lord. A heathen like you probably won't understand that, but I can assure you there was no question of swearing. It was just an intense wish."

Vledder remained silent.

Bram Weelen, the police photographer entered the room. He placed his heavy aluminum case on the floor and wiped the sweat from his forehead. He gave DeKok a pained look.

"You are certainly all over the place. You're almost in Oldkerk here. Surely this is a job for the Twenty-third? What are you doing here? I thought you belonged to Warmoes Street."

"We could ask you the same," said Vledder. "You belong in the city."

"I came because the Twenty-third does not have a photographer available at the moment. I was next on the call list, so here I am. I thought everyone else was coming from the Twenty-third. You still haven't answered my question."

DeKok grimaced.

"We're here to investigate the murders of the geese," he

said somberly. "Mrs. Bildijk's is an influential woman. Her geese were murdered, so we've had to come out to the provinces."

Weelen nodded. He completely understood how DeKok would refer to the farthest suburb of Amsterdam as the 'provinces.' A real Amsterdammer considered Amsterdam the only city in the Netherlands. The rest of the country was ancillary, as well. Never mind that Rotterdam is the largest, busiest, harbor in the world and The Hague is the seat of the country's government.

"I saw those animals ... on the lawn," said Weelen. "I thought it very strange ... maybe the result of parrot fever, or something."

DeKok shook his head, smiling.

"They were probably poisoned." He pointed at the corpse of the old gardener. "And now that they have also killed this poor, honest fellow, I'm in the middle of a real mess."

"Was he so decent?"

"I think so." DeKok indicated the dilapidated surroundings. "People who stay in service out of loyalty and remain poor usually are honest."

"Or not so bright," grinned Weelen.

He opened his aluminum case and extracted a Hasselblad camera. He mounted some additional gadgets and started to take his pictures. He photographed the surroundings, the corpse from several angles, and then lowered his camera.

"Any particular requests?" he asked DeKok.

"Yes, I want a few sharp close-ups of the wound."

Weelen looked closely at the wound and pursed his lips, considering.

"I'll give them to you in black and white and in color." He bent down and exchanged cameras. "Black and white," he explained as he snapped away. He then picked up the original camera and did something to the lens. He took more pictures.

"Done," he said after a while. "Is that it?"

DeKok rubbed his chin.

"If it's not too much trouble, I would like you to come back during the day tomorrow. I'd like some pictures outside. Could I get both the big house and this coach house from all sides? It would be good to get a view from here to the gate and back, and the same from the other house."

"No problem, but I cannot get the finished pictures to you before tomorrow night."

"All right, thank you."

A man came into the room, followed by two paramedics with a stretcher.

"Ah, doctor," began DeKok. Then he paused, took a closer look at the man and said: "You're not Dr. Koning."

"That's right," answered the man. "My name is Han, Jacob Han. I'm the coroner for Oldkerk and surroundings, which includes this part of Amsterdam."

"I see," said DeKok. "But doctor I want the body transported to Amsterdam, for Dr. Rusteloos."

"No problem, my men will be happy to deliver it wherever you want."

At this point a boy of sixteen squeezed past the paramedics and stopped in front of DeKok.

"Aunt asks you to hurry up ... she wants you to start the interviews in the house. The family is getting tired."

Something seemed to snap inside DeKok. He felt the rage mounting inside him. He put his hands in his pockets and curled them into fists. With difficulty he managed to control the rage that threatened to make him do something rash.

"You tell your aunt," he began in a loud voice. Then he

stopped, took a deep breath and continued in a more normal voice. "Tell your aunt this for me. Now that Willem is sleeping for all eternity, the family can stay awake a little longer."

The boy, Paul, disappeared.

Dr. Han stretched out his hand to DeKok.

"That was very good," he laughed, as they shook hands. "Very good, Inspector. I will remember that. It's a pleasure to finally work with you."

The coroner walked over to the man in the rattan chair. He carefully studied the wound and then looked up.

"This man is dead," he announced.

"Thank you, doctor," answered DeKok formally. Under Dutch law the person had only now officially become a corpse.

The coroner motioned to the paramedics.

"Wait outside," he said. "The inspector will let you know when and where to take the body as soon as they have finished."

"Oh, they can take the body now," said DeKok. "Vledder will tell them where to take it."

"Very well," answered the doctor, nodding to his men. Then he turned to DeKok. "As you may know, Inspector, we coroners keep in close contact. We're aware this is not the first elderly person to suffer a mortal wound to the head recently. There have been a number of cases."

Vledder overheard the remark. Weelen, who had just finished closing his suitcase, also listened. DeKok looked around and despite the sparse light, he clearly saw the grim faces of the men around him.

"Igor," murmured DeKok, "Igor Stablinsky."

Bram Weelen had left in his usual boisterous manner. The dispassionate paramedics had left with the body. Dr. Han had left with them. Except for the dactyloscopist, the rest of the forensic team had not yet arrived, so DeKok sank down in one of the rattan chairs. He felt desolate and exhausted. He pulled up a sleeve and looked at his watch. It was just a little past midnight and he wondered where the forensic team could be. He knew that the Bildijk family was waiting for him in the big house. He felt reluctant to renew his confrontation with the slippery Ivo and his patronizing aunt. Idly he watched the fingerprint man work with his powders and brushes. He seemed competent enough, but DeKok longed for Kruger, his usual support in such cases. He also longed to return to his comfort zone in the familiar, inner city. It was the place he considered Amsterdam 'proper.'

"Everything here's unusable," grumbled Tees, the dactyloscopist from the Twenty-third Precinct. "The surfaces are either too rough, or too greasy. Some of it looks like it's never been cleaned. I can't find a decent print."

Gingerly DeKok rubbed his calves. Much to his surprise he found them pain-free, soft, and supple. He suffered hellish pain in his legs; the stress of the job exacerbated the condition. He noticed his pain worsen when he took a wrong turn, or despaired of finding answers. Vledder watched the gesture from across the room. He sighed a small sigh of relief as he realized DeKok's legs were not hurting this time.

DeKok stood up and turned to Vledder.

"When he's finished here," he said pointing at Tees, "just seal everything up. If the rest of the team shows up, they'll know what they have to do. If not, they can find us. Frankly, I think the rest of the team is as elusive as the people who were supposed to remove the geese."

Vledder shrugged. He was determined not to take responsibility for the performance, or non-performance, of any team from the suburbs.

"All right," said Vledder. "I already took the tape and seals out of the car."

DeKok nodded and waved a thumb over his shoulder.

"I'll start next door," he said. He said a friendly goodbye to the fingerprint expert and left the room.

One step at a time, he cautiously descended the dark staircase. He could hear the rats shuffling around the corners of the coach house. Old Willem, he thought cynically, really had needed the strychnine.

He exited through the large doors. The pale moonlight threw long shadows behind the parked cars. Light was still streaming through all the windows in the mansion.

Suddenly he heard a whisper.

"Psst … psst."

DeKok's immediate reaction was to lower his profile, then he concentrated his gaze in the direction of the sound.

From the shadow thrown by a Volvo appeared a puny figure. It approached the inspector slowly.

"Psst … I'm Penny … do you remember? I'm staying here with my two brothers."

With a sigh DeKok rose to his full height and sounded a relieved laugh.

"Penny Miller?"

The child nodded.

"Yes, that's me. My mother's name is Irmgard and if Aunt Isolde dies, we'll inherit a lot of money."

"That's nice."

The child gave him a hard look.

"You're Inspector DeKok, a police officer. I've read

about you ... about murders and things ... and I want to help you."

She shuffled closer. She wore a long coat over her pajamas and her small feet were stuck in slippers that were too large for her. DeKok looked at her feet.

"Mother's," explained the child.

A worried look came into DeKok's eyes.

"How long have you been waiting here?"

She pulled the coat tighter around herself.

"About half an hour, I think. I saw the others leave, the stretcher too. I thought it was very sad about Uncle Willem. I liked Uncle Willem; he was nice. He was always willing to play with us. He was good to me and my brothers, while we visited our aunt during summer vacations."

DeKok nodded.

"Why did you not stay with the others in the living room?"

She shook her head decisively.

"Inside ... where the others are ... I wouldn't dare say it."

"What?"

She made a gesture, both childish and mature beyond her years.

"I know who did it."

DeKok leaned closer, speaking very quietly.

"And this you are certain you know?"

She nodded with conviction.

"Yes, Uncle Izaak ... I saw him walking outside with a stick, and ..."

Despite his relaxed posture, DeKok was agitated. He glanced

at the green light of the communication gear. The light cast eerie shadows on his face. With an exasperated sigh he pushed his lower lip forward.

"What ... and?" he asked, irritation in his voice.

Vledder made a soothing gesture.

"Did the interrogations help us at all?"

DeKok shook his head slowly.

"Apparently the death of Willem took them all by surprise. At least it stifled any criticism about my handling of the case. When I came in, old lady Bildijk stood, leaning on a stick, surrounded by her family. She said that she preferred to stand during our interview. Ivo had to support her, or she would have toppled over."

"Didn't you find that strange?"

"Yes, but I ignored it. She didn't say a word about the threatening letters, not a word about my not arresting her gardener. Just a forceful demand to find the murderer in the shortest possible time with every means at my disposal."

Vledder barked a short laugh.

"What about the others?"

DeKok shrugged.

"Nothing. Ivo stuck to his story. There was a heated discussion with the gardener. The letters and I were the main subjects. The conversation ended around ten o'clock, and everyone claims to have gone straight to bed at that rather early hour. Aunt Isolde had called Ivo to her room over the house phone around eleven thirty and ordered him to talk once more to Willem about the letters."

"Then what?"

DeKok sighed a long-suffering sigh.

"Ivo supposedly got dressed reluctantly, and went to the coach house. The light in Willem's room was on. He went upstairs with no inkling of what he was about to find. Next, he saw Willem in his chair with his bashed-in skull. He ran back to Aunt Isolde's room and told her what had happened. Together they decided to call the police. A little later Isolde became curious and ordered Ivo to search Willem's room."

Vledder nodded to himself.

"Where we found him and thwarted his search."

For a while they drove along in silence. There was no traffic on the road along the river. The houses were far apart and dark. In the distance, a long stream of headlights raced across the Amstel Bridge in the direction of Utrecht and points east.

Vledder broke the silence.

"But what about Penny's tale?"

DeKok hesitated, searched his pockets, and found a toffee. He unwrapped it and placed the wrapper in the ashtray. He inspected the sweet as if he had never seen anything like it. Then he popped it in his mouth. He chewed a few times before he answered.

"I didn't dare bring it up," he said finally.

Vledder showed amazement.

"Why not?"

DeKok rubbed the back of his neck.

"As long as I don't understand what's happening ... and I don't understand a thing, least of all the motive. I don't want to endanger the child needlessly. In fact, it would be best not to need her at all. She won't say a word to anyone. We made a pact to keep the secret just between the two of us." He paused and rubbed the back of his neck again. "Of course," he continued, "I asked them all, including Izaak, where they were between the time they went to bed and the time they were called out of their beds by the old lady."

"And?"

"They claimed to be asleep."

"Izaak, too?"

"Yes."

"But the little girl saw him behind the house?"

"Yes, she had to go to the bathroom. As she passed the window in the hallway, she saw Izaak slinking through the garden.

"Slinking?"

"Her words. She's pretty smart for a little girl. During the interrogations in the living room, she just said she had been asleep. Didn't elaborate, so you wouldn't have pursued it further. It made it easy for me to dismiss her almost immediately."

"Did she see any blood spots on Izaak?"

DeKok shook his head wearily.

"It would have been too dark to see that sort of detail, besides, there were no blood spots. Willem was hit once, though with great force. There would have been no splatter pattern. The pattern comes after the second, or repeated blows. And that didn't happen. Perhaps there was blood on the weapon, but I couldn't find that."

"So, a whole lot of nothing."

"Yes. You may find something tomorrow, in the daylight. Bram is going to be there anyway, to make some more pictures. Who knows, the technical service may have arrived by then. You can also look for footprints. It was pitch black, so I didn't attempt to find prints with my flashlight."

DeKok remained silent, except for the noisy sucking on his toffee. They had already reached the inner city before he broke the silence.

"Any fingerprints, or anything else useful?"

Vledder merely shook his head. He looked tired.

"It's about time for me to find my bed," he yawned as he pulled the car into the parking slot nearby. Shortly thereafter they entered the station house.

The watch commander looked up from his register and yelled at DeKok in his usual loud voice.

"That guy has been here again!"

"What guy?" asked DeKok.

"The fat drug dealer, " said Meindert Post. "He waited for over an hour for you guys."

"Crazy Chris. What did he want?"

"I asked him the same thing," grinned Post. "He took his sweet time to finally give me a message."

"Well, what was the message?," asked DeKok impatiently.

Meindert Post fished a piece of paper from a pile on one side of his desk.

"Here it is. The German whore is back, Inge." He handed the paper to DeKok. "See, one nine seven Long Leiden Side Street."

DeKok crammed the piece of paper into his coat pocket and turned around.

Dazed and a bit glassy eyed Vledder followed him.

"Where are you going?"

"Long Leiden Side Street."

Vledder looked pained.

"But I need sleep."

DeKok nodded. His watery blue eyes were wreathed in red.

"Me too, but I won't sleep peacefully until I've got Igor behind bars again."

10

Long Leiden Side Street was long, narrow, and dark. Toward the end, near Mirror Canal, there were no street lamps. DeKok managed to park the car, askew and after a number of bumps, between two cars. He did not like to drive. By his own admission he was the worst driver in the Netherlands, probably in all of Europe. The straight stick in the ancient VW was his particular nemesis. It was worn and crotchety. Combined with the slippery old clutch, it took maximum effort to get the car in the proper gear. It usually took several tries.

With a sigh, DeKok turned off the headlights. Sweat beaded on his forehead. He wiped his face with a sleeve and turned off the ignition. He slid down in the seat with a feeling of relief.

Vledder gave him a sleepy look. The young man was obviously fatigued. It was the reason DeKok had driven himself. Vledder had been so sleepy he even lacked the energy to make his usual comments about DeKok's driving ability. "Can't find 'em, grind 'em," was one of his more innocuous remarks when DeKok was fighting the gears. Vledder was convinced the two of them were still saddled with this ancient relic, simply because their bosses knew DeKok occasionally drove.

"Did we make it?" asked Vledder.

DeKok pointed through the windshield.

"Yes," answered DeKok testily, "right across the street, just a few doors down. Number one hundred and ninety-seven."

"Are we going in?"

"No." DeKok shook his head. "I know these houses along here. It is easy to miscalculate around here. I have done it myself. Literally anyone can find an escape route from the alley side to anywhere. We'd never make an arrest with just two officers. Besides," he added ruefully, "I'm too old to start chasing over these rooftops and crumbling walls."

Vledder grinned. He was feeling more alert.

"So, why did we make the trip? What's our next move?"

"We wait."

"Until our friend Igor comes whistling through the front door and ask us to please arrest him?"

"I see you're getting your second wind," said DeKok, noting the sarcastic words as well as the tone in Vledder's voice.

"Sorry, but what else can we do?"

DeKok took a deep breath.

"The information from Crazy Chris is current," the old sleuth explained patiently. "Chris lives only a few houses down the street. It's possible she would call him first, to get a fresh fix. Igor has been asking after Inge, but her friends weren't in a mood to cooperate. It will take some time before Igor emerges."

Vledder yawned.

"He could take days to show."

DeKok smiled.

"Don't worry, Inge will have to hit the streets very soon to get enough money for her next fix, if nothing else. The bush telephone in the underworld is very fast ... and usually accurate." He gestured across the street. "We may even be too late."

"How's that?"

"Maybe Igor has been here already and dragged her away."

"Against her will?"

"If necessary."

"But why?"

"Perhaps Igor has decided she knows too much."

It started to get warm inside the car. DeKok threw his hat on the rear seat. Condensation started to form on the windows and Vledder cracked the window on his side and loosened his tie.

"Do you think Igor bludgeoned old Willem?"

"It was a typical Igor murder," said DeKok after a moment's thought. "He approaches his victim from behind and a deals a single blow to the head. There's just one deviation."

"Oh?"

"Yes, the gardener wasn't Igor's usual victim—he didn't own anything of value."

DeKok cleaned the window on his side of the car by wiping a sleeve across the condensation. He thought he saw a movement across the street. He discovered a man who had his collar pulled up high and his hat pulled down in his eyes. He stopped in front of number one hundred ninety-seven and rang the doorbell.

Vledder had noticed the same thing and sat up suddenly.

"Igor?" he whispered to DeKok.

"No, I'd recognize him anywhere."

A few seconds later, a scantily dressed woman opened the door. The light from inside fell on the head of the man in front of the door. The thinning hair fit like an oily cap.

"Izaak Bildijk," panted Vledder. He straightened his tie and was ready to get out of the car. DeKok placed a restraining hand on the young man's arm.

"Wait," said DeKok.

"But ... but ..." stammered Vledder.

DeKok made an apologetic gesture.

"It's not against the law in Amsterdam for a single male to visit a prostitute."

Vledder grinned without mirth.

"But ... eh, he was also in the garden."

DeKok nodded resignedly.

"Yes, Izaak has been a busy boy."

"How did the autopsy go?"

Vledder smirked.

"I think it's the first time I've seen Dr. Rusteloos angry."

"What did he do—slice his finger with a scalpel?"

Smiling, Vledder shook his head.

"No, it was about the old gardener's head wound. Dr. Rusteloos remarked he's seen a number of these blunt trauma wounds lately. I told him that we were after Igor Stablinsky for that very reason. I mentioned Igor had been in custody, but we'd let him escape."

"And that made him angry?"

Vledder nodded, no longer amused.

"Dr. Rusteloos was incensed. He's all about accountability for people who are responsible for the escape of dangerous criminals. He wants them punished for the felonies their escapees commit."

DeKok pursed his lips in thought.

"At first blush, I like it. On a practical level no government will pass a law to try neglectful jailers in the criminal courts." He looked closely at Vledder. "How are you feeling? Did you get some rest last night?"

Vledder nodded.

"I'm glad you finally decided to send me home. I was really drained. But how did you get home after I took the car?"

"I waited until Izaak came out again. I followed him on foot. His path led me to Princes Canal where his car was parked. I presume he went back to Happy Lake from there."

"And what about Igor?"

"Trail's gone cold."

Vledder rummaged in a desk drawer and took out a large yellow envelope.

"From the King's Procurator in Antwerp," he explained.

DeKok looked nonplussed.

"Antwerp?" he questioned with raised eyebrows.

Vledder waited a few seconds to see if DeKok's eyebrows would perform their unusual gymnastics. When that did not happen, he answered DeKok's question.

"Remember when you asked me to check out the nephews and the niece of Mrs. Bildijk? I started right away."

"Aha," said DeKok, "so I did. What did you find out?"

Vledder opened the envelope and scanned the papers he pulled from the envelope. He switched on his computer absent mindedly, and fanned the papers out on his desk. His hands reached for his keyboard.

"Forget that for the moment," prompted DeKok. "Give me the gist of it."

"Sorry," answered Vledder and picked up one of the

papers. His eyes scanned down the page. "Well," he said after a brief pause, "it seems Ivo Bildijk's hair isn't the only greasy thing about him. He's not the solid citizen he appears to be. Over the last few years he's been arrested several times for duplicity and tax fraud."

"Convictions?"

Vledder smiled wryly.

"Every time either a dismissal, or what the Belgians call 'discharge from prosecution.' Ivo is as slippery as an eel. Never any convincing evidence against him."

"What does he do in Antwerp?"

"He's president and owner of a contracting firm."

"How's business?"

Vledder shook his head slowly as he read.

"Business is bad. According to this, Ivo is going belly up. Last week he petitioned the court for bankruptcy protection, to keep the wolves at bay."

This time DeKok's eyebrows did start a life of their own. They rippled in ways that made one suspect two hairy caterpillars had come to life on his forehead. Unfortunately, Vledder was still engrossed in the papers and did not see the phenomenon.

"In that case Aunt Isolde's inheritance would be more than welcome," remarked DeKok.

"Yes," said Vledder thoughtfully, "but she has to die first."

DeKok stood up and walked over to the peg where he kept his raincoat. He put it on and placed his little hat on his head. He motioned for Vledder to follow.

"Where are we going?" asked Vledder as he hastily crammed the papers back in the envelope.

"We're going to Bussum," answered DeKok. The death

of that old gardener is incomprehensible. Where could such a seemingly senseless killing fit into the scheme of things? We just don't know enough. That's why I want to talk to Uncle Immanuel."

"But Immanuel suffers from senile dementia," said Vledder as he closed the drawer in which he had stowed the envelope.

DeKok nodded pensively.

"So says the family. But a slight eccentricity is often the best way for an older person to defend against young, energetic schemers." He smiled. "Uncle Immanuel is not just very well off, he is smart enough to have remained that way."

Vledder looked as if he had just made a new discovery.

"You mean his nephews and nieces ..." He did not finish the sentence. The phone on DeKok's desk started ringing.

Vledder walked over and picked up the receiver. DeKok watched from a distance. He saw his partner's face pale. Slowly DeKok came closer. Vledder replaced the receiver and looked at DeKok.

"Izaak," murmured Vledder.

"What's the matter with Izaak," asked DeKok, suspecting the answer.

Vledder swallowed with difficulty.

"Izaak is dead, he was found in his chair."

DeKok looked around the room with a photographer's eye. He was able to absorb any surroundings and store an image in his memory with the accuracy of a computer. He had total recall. Many times DeKok had relied more on his memory than anything else to solve his cases. It was a useful talent. He looked at the old-fashioned espagnolette closure of the

French doors. Inside the room, there was an equally old-fashioned, unused bed and a marble-topped table containing a Delft blue bowl and watering jug. The electrical wires were wall-mounted on small ceramic pods and ran parallel to each other, about two inches apart. The room may last have been modernized around the turn of the century, definitely before the First World War.

Izaak Bildijk's corpse leaned in a heavy oak chair. The chair's back and armrests had been fitted with padded leather, secured by intricately designed brass tacks. The corpse was dressed in the same clothes DeKok had observed the previous night, minus the suit coat. The coat hung from a peg on the inside of the door.

DeKok looked closely at the corpse. From just below the hairline a line of coagulated blood ran down next to the left ear. A small puddle of black blood obliterated the elaborate pattern of an Ispahan carpet. Izaak's clear blue eyes were wide open with an expression of terror. He looked as though he had momentarily comprehended what was happening. The murderer had dealt him a single, fatal blow from the back. The victim had been unaware of his killer's approach.

DeKok did not feel the need, as in the case of old Willem, to close the eyes of the corpse. In fact, he was numb. He searched his conscience, surprised. Izaak's death left him unmoved. It was just another murder, one of so many. He wondered if he had lost his sensitivity, if he had become just another calculating machine. It had always worried him. He felt that when a policeman lost his compassion, his effectiveness went with it. It was critical to remain human. He shrugged the uneasy feeling away and looked at Ivo Bildijk.

Bildijk was standing behind the chair. Again DeKok reflected how little the brothers resembled each other. He compared the face of the deceased with that of Ivo, but saw no family resemblance. He gestured toward the corpse.

"Who discovered him?" asked DeKok.

Ivo Bildijk swallowed and licked dry lips.

"I did," he said hoarsely.

"You seem to have a knack for discovering dead bodies." It sounded scathing. "What time did you discover him?"

"It was near noon."

DeKok looked at his watch.

"About forty-five minutes ago?"

"Just about."

"This man has been dead for hours." DeKok pointed at the corpse. "There is virtually no rigor mortis. Did nobody think to check on him sooner?" His voice was sardonic. "There are so many of you in the house."

Ivo did not answer at once. He rummaged in a side pocket, took out a small piece of paper, and offered it to DeKok.

"This was pinned to the outside of his door."

DeKok accepted the note and read the handwritten text out loud: ""Please do not call me for breakfast."" He looked at Ivo. "His handwriting?" he asked.

Ivo Bildijk nodded.

"We think he left late last night, after you left. He must have returned even later."

"And therefore he pinned this to the door," DeKok held up the note, "to ensure that he would get a few hours rest?"

"It seems reasonable."

The inspector pointed at the unused bed, still made up in military precision.

"He did not get a lot of rest, after all." He looked sharply at Ivo. "Do you have any idea where he could have been, last night?"

"No."

"Did he say anything to anybody?"

"Izaak and I were never close, even as children. Our characters were too different. Each of us always preferred to go his own way. We had our own boyhood friends and acquaintances, rather than mutual associates. As we matured, we drifted even further apart. I moved to Antwerp and Izaak settled in Oldkerk."

DeKok pounced. "It was from Oldkerk the threatening letters were mailed," he remarked.

Ivo's mouth pulled into a wry smile.

"A remarkable coincidence, don't you find?"

"You think so?"

Ivo shrugged, annoyed.

"In any event, I don't want to discuss Willem's involvement again."

DeKok was getting irritated. His voice sounded harsh.

"Willem's involvement in what?" he demanded.

"His coincidental trips to Oldkerk when someone mailed the threatening letters," answered Ivo, rubbing his hands together as though he were washing them. "His animosity toward my aunt," he continued. "We have discussed that business among ourselves ... among the family." He made conclusive gesture. "Those discussions ended with Willem's death."

"*Not* for me," asserted DeKok vehemently. "As far as I'm concerned the discussions have just begun. I feel in my bones Willem was murdered to no end, unnecessarily." He smiled grimly. "As if there could be such a thing as a *necessary* murder."

"Ach," said Ivo nonchalantly, "the gardener was old and troublesome. In fact, he'd long since become a waste of space."

The contempt and callousness in Ivo's voice caused something within DeKok to snap. He strode past the chair with the corpse and planted himself directly in front of Ivo. Slowly, menacingly, he leaned forward and brought his face within inches of the now frightened Ivo Bildijk. DeKok became overcome with a combination of disgust, abhorrence, and loathing for the plump, obsequious man before him. He struggled with a sudden urge to pound his greasy face to a pulp. Fortunately DeKok recognized the trigger of berserk rage that sometimes overcomes the usually placid Dutch people. It was almost a national curse. He shook a trembling index finger in front of Ivo's face.

"If one of you … because of some insane notion of taking the law in your own hands … if one of you has killed that old man, I'll …"

He stopped suddenly and took a deep breath. His rage began to subside. Slowly he lowered his arm and pressed the nails of his fingers into his palms.

The shiny face of Ivo Bildijk was distorted by an ugly grin as he pointed to the dead body of his brother.

"Tell me, Inspector, what sort of insanity explains this?"

11

Two stoic men from the municipal morgue placed the corpse of Ivo Bildijk inside the body bag and strapped the bag to the stretcher. With a slightly swaying gait, the stretcher between them, they left.

As DeKok watched them leave he felt a stirring of conscience. Oddly, it felt good. Seeing Izaak leave for good, DeKok felt a stir of conscience and compassion he had not felt as he first looked down at the unfortunate man's corpse. He became suddenly consumed with this death. It was no longer a routine event.

Vledder accompanied the paramedics, opening and closing doors for them. No family members were anywhere to be seen. They had gathered in the somber living room.

Bram Weelen, the photographer, had already left. He had been recalled to Amsterdam where other cases were waiting for him. Just DeKok's favorite fingerprint expert, Kruger, lingered. The technical team from the Twenty-third Precinct never materialized. This allowed DeKok to insist police headquarters in Amsterdam provide him with his usual support group. It would be easier to work with people he knew and respected. He watched as Kruger re-packed his case, preparatory to leaving.

"With this kind of situation," said Kruger sadly, "you never find anything. Just smears and prints from the residents."

He pointed at the now empty chair. "I'll get his prints in the morgue."

"You want to make sure he's who he is?" replied DeKok, "But I don't think you'll find his prints on file. He was, how shall I put it … a more or less respectable man."

"We're all more or less proper citizens," commented Kruger, "but I'll just make sure."

DeKok nodded, his thoughts already elsewhere. Vledder came back and asked Kruger a question.

"Are you prepared to make casts of footprints?"

"Yes, I have the stuff in the car. Did you find something?"

Vledder turned to DeKok.

"Because Bram had to leave so quickly, I took a look around on my own. There are definite footprints in the garden, on the edge of the path," he pointed at the window. "They lead from here to a window a few rooms down."

"Which room?"

"Isolde's room."

DeKok rubbed his chin thoughtfully. A fleeting little smile appeared.

"In that case Penny may indeed have seen Uncle Izaak in the garden last night." He looked up. "Do the footsteps go anywhere else?"

Vledder shook his head.

"They end in front of the old lady's room. There they are a bit smudged and the toes of the shoes are deeper, as if someone stood tip-toe to look inside."

"Fine," said DeKok. "What else?"

"I retraced the footsteps to here."

"This room."

"Exactly, I found some mud from the flower beds on the

tiles in front of the doors." Vledder pointed at the French doors.

"Did you find a stick?"

Vledder shrugged.

"There are lots of bushes close to the house. It might be there, somewhere. I actually looked only at the footsteps. The forensic team may find it, if it's there."

"Were there signs of a break-in?"

Vledder shook his head resolutely.

"Not that I could see. All the windows of the house, even those in the upper level, are intact. No scratches or signs of forcible entry. And the security is quite adequate ... bolts, dead-bolts, even some chains." He looked at DeKok with an apologetic smile. "No chance for Igor to get in," he added slowly.

DeKok stared into the distance.

"Unless ... unless someone from the inside let him in."

They were all together in the cheerless living room with the view of the meadow. Isolde Bildijk in the center, stiff and straight in her ornate "throne." Her nephew Ivo stood to her right, looking the part of the evil vizier to his monarch. His puffy hand rested on a projection from the back of the chair.

DeKok approached slowly, insolently.

As before, Irmgard was seated on the wide bench to the left. Her children were again lined up behind her. Everything was the same as the previous day, except that Izaak was missing. Vledder glanced at Penny. The little girl wore the same red velvet dress. She winked at DeKok.

DeKok ignored it, did not give any indication that he had seen anything. He stopped in front of Isolde's throne and briefly bowed his head.

"I wish to express my ... eh, my sympathies regarding the sudden loss of your nephew, Izaak," he said formally. "It must have been a cruel blow for you, so shortly after the loss of your dedicated gardener."

Mrs. Bildijk pressed her lips together in disapproval.

"The gardener was a servant," she said sharply, "an inferior. Izaak was a highly regarded member of my family."

DeKok nodded to himself as if he had just confirmed something.

"That distinction does not count as far as I'm concerned. And I assure you no judge will give greater weight to one life than to the other, when I deliver the murderer to justice."

Isolde Bildijk shook her head.

"Our values differ," she said with a resigned tone in her voice. "I've been sorely disappointed in your conduct in this matter, Inspector." She sighed deeply. "And you came highly recommended as an excellent detective."

Once again DeKok nodded to himself. The expression on his face did not change.

"Perhaps 'some' overestimate my capabilities." He leaned closer. "But I *will* catch the killer."

Isolde Bildijk smiled condescendingly.

"I'd like to know when that will be?" she demanded.

DeKok looked at her with a penetrating look.

"It will be when I have finished my work—when I have sufficient evidence to convict."

This time she gave a short, barking, derisive laugh. It sounded unpleasant and insulting.

"Evidence! Why would you bother with that? I had evidence against my gardener and you refused to take him into police custody."

DeKok remained passive.

"I regret it more than I can say," he said evenly. "If I had arrested him he might still be alive … he would not have been executed."

Isolde Bildijk snorted. Her nostrils trembled and her eyes had a malicious light in them.

"What are you trying to insinuate?"

"His murderer was a Bildijk."

Vledder drove away from the coach house with so much speed the gravel spun away from the rear wheels. He looked at DeKok with a puzzled face.

"What made you say that?"

"Eh?"

"The gardener has been murdered by a Bildijk."

DeKok sat up straighter and pointed out the window.

"Those carcasses are still there," he censured.

"I have phoned them again," Vledder apologized. "Apparently they have had no time to collect the birds." As he negotiated the gate he remained silent. Once they were on the road, he spoke again.

"But you still haven't answered my question."

DeKok smiled as he unearthed a peppermint from his breast pocket. He dusted it off and put it in his mouth. Only then did he turn to Vledder.

"It was a gut reaction," admitted DeKok. He grinned boyishly. "It was precipitated, more or less, by the irritating behavior of that wicked old woman." He sighed. "Happy Lake is like a keg about to burst. It's full of passions and contrasting emotions. I wanted to force a reaction … any reaction."

"Well, even so," said Vledder, "we're in a jam. Our case

is at a dead-end. I hope something happens soon, or we'll never solve it."

"You don't think two murders are enough?"

The young inspector shook his head.

"That's not what I mean. Every murder is one too many. Like you, the murder of old Willem troubles me the most. I certainly cannot fit the pieces of this puzzle together, but I'm also very affected by the senseless waste of his death. If we could limit ourselves to the murder of Izaak, it would be easy to decide on a motive."

"I'm listening," said DeKok.

Vledder drove the car onto the shoulder and switched off the engine. He turned toward DeKok.

"Irmgard, Ivo, and Izaak had motive," he began, enthusiastically. "They're all hot for the inheritance they expect from Aunt Isolde. To make her nervous, one of them sends her threatening letters."

"It suited their purpose to have the gardener falsely accused."

Vledder nodded.

"Next, they decide to kill the geese she kept for protection."

"Again, the gardener is fingered for the despicable act."

"Yes," said Vledder impatiently. "But you see what happens? The threats and the death of the geese set off an alarm. Isolde issues an emergency invitation to the heirs to come to Happy Lake. They gather, ostensibly, to help protect and support her during this distressing time."

DeKok was genuinely interested.

"You're doing very well ... go on."

"Izaak, tired of waiting, decides on his own to hasten the departure of his aunt."

"So the others did not know?"

"No ... that is ... they didn't have to know.

"But they would profit."

Vledder shrugged a bit uncertainly.

"Well, maybe they conspired. Or maybe Izaak did not take them into account ... perhaps his own financial difficulties were too pressing. Maybe he figured his share of the loot would be sufficient for his needs."

DeKok gave his colleague a long, thoughtful look.

"But why Izaak," he asked finally.

Vledder sighed at so much incomprehension.

"Think about the footsteps in the garden that ended at Isolde's bedroom. And think of what the little girl told you. She saw Izaak walking around with a stick."

DeKok smiled politely.

"It sounds reasonable, but Aunt Isolde is still safe and sound on her throne in the living room."

"Something went wrong," said Vledder.

"What?"

Vledder was getting irritated.

"I don't know," he said. "It could have been a matter of control ... of direction. Perhaps somebody else had the same idea and bashed in the wrong skull." He remained silent for a moment and pressed his lips together while he made an obstinate gesture toward his older colleague. "One thing I know for sure," he continued doggedly, "one of these days the carefully coiffed head of Aunt Isolde will roll. I'm certain of that."

12

As they reached the city, they passed the old Palace of Justice. It looked terrible, all covered with graffiti. DeKok looked at it. It pained him to see the old, venerable building so neglected. He saw it as a sign of the times. Law and justice were daily denigrated, the symbols of law and justice vandalized.

DeKok was thinking out loud. "There is some soul of goodness in things evil. Would men observantly distill it out."

"What?" asked Vledder. "Is that a quotation?"

DeKok gestured at the old building.

"I was just thinking about right, justice, and the law and the low esteem in which they are kept." He grinned sadly. "The quote is from Shakespeare's *Henry V.*"

"Well at least he held out some hope," laughed Vledder.

"Maybe, but what about 'There's small choice in rotten apples?'"

"He didn't say that."

"Oh, yes. It's in *The Taming of the Shrew.*"

"My, you're in a pessimistic mood."

"On the contrary, in a pessimistic mood, I would have said, 'Destroy the seed of evil, or it will grow up to your ruin.'" He paused and then he said: "It means to kill evil at birth, or it will return with a vengeance. It's from Aesop," he added.

"Rather drastic, I think. But I thought Aesop just wrote fables."

"This is from a fable, *The Swallow and the Other Birds.*"

Vledder seemed dumbfounded by so much erudition and they continued in silence.

Long Leiden Side Street looked less sinister in the daylight. The furtive movement of shadowy figures had dissolved. Vledder parked close to number one hundred ninety-seven and they got out of the car. Vledder locked the doors and followed DeKok.

"Why are we here?"

"We're looking for German Inge."

"I see. Of course, you're not going to visit Crazy Chris, not during the day." He grimaced. "Do you really expect German Inge to tell you where to find Igor?"

DeKok shook his head.

"After Willem's death, I was blindsided by Izaak's demise. I had not foreseen anything like it. I'm wondering whether Izaak's visit here last night was only for sex."

"But what other reason could there be?"

DeKok did not answer. He stopped in front of the door. He pulled a little brass instrument from his pocket ... once a present from an ex-burglar. It allowed him to open virtually any lock.

Vledder shook his head in disapproval.

"You can't do that," he protested. "Not in the middle of the day, in broad daylight. Besides, she's probably home. The girls usually don't start work until the evening."

DeKok seemed deaf. He looked at the lock and then selected a particular combination of extensions from the brass cylinder. Within a few seconds the lock opened and he pushed against the door. It moved.

"You must never underestimate the element of surprise during an investigation," lectured DeKok as he replaced the small instrument in his pocket.

Vledder let out a long-suffering sigh.

"But this is breaking and entering, DeKok," he remon-strated. "It is burglary. One of these days you'll get in a lot of trouble." He sounded worried.

His older colleague grinned naughtily. His face looked cheerful as if he had just won a prize. His conscience was not bothering him a bit.

"I can't help it," he said with a straight face, "if German Inge doesn't keep her door locked. Some people are very careless."

Vledder did not appreciate the joke. His face stern, he followed DeKok into the dark corridor. The only light came from a small window over the front door that they closed behind them.

DeKok signaled Vledder to walk to the end of the corridor.

"There's a small kitchen with a back door. The door leads to a tiny backyard, surrounded by a wall. No matter who tries to leave that way ... you stop him, or her."

Vledder nodded and disappeared toward the back of the house.

On the left side of the corridor a door was ajar. DeKok entered carefully and found himself in a long, narrow room. Near the center, against the wall, was a young woman asleep in a double bed. Despite the streaked make-up, DeKok rec-ognized her as the woman who had received Izaak Bildijk the previous night. He loosened his coat, placed a bra, a pair of panties, and some stockings on a different chair and sat down in the chair next to the bed. His attitude was calm and relaxed, as if he often came for a visit.

Meanwhile he listened for noises, but the old house was quiet. On the floor above he heard light footsteps and the sound of a radio. He could barely hear Vledder rummaging around in the kitchen.

He let his eyes wander around the room. On the street side, a small table held a telephone. A late-model television set sat on the floor next to the table. With the exception of the TV, the furnishings looked to be the products of forays to flea markets. The bed was none too clean, either. The dingy, gray sheets and pillowcases had not been washed for weeks. They lent a rancid odor to the room. Suddenly squeamish, DeKok wondered how Izaak could have stayed here as long as he did.

After a few minutes the woman on the bed started to toss and turn. It seemed she was aware of his presence in the room. She sat bolt upright in the bed and stared at DeKok with wild eyes.

"Who, who are *you?* How did you get in? What are you doing here?"

DeKok gave her his best smile.

"That's too many," he said cheerfully. "That's three questions all at once." He leaned forward and stretched out his hand to the woman. "My name is DeKok ... with kay-oh-kay. I'm a police inspector."

German Inge took his hand and shook it briefly. Then she fell back on the pillow.

"A cop," she said. It sounded disillusioned. "I've already reported myself. I told you I'm no longer missing."

DeKok shook his head.

"That's not why I'm here."

She raised herself again to a seated position, baring her breasts.

"Then what do you want?"

DeKok gave her an admiring look.

"For a *German* Inge, you speak excellent Dutch."

She shrugged her shoulders.

"My mother … mother is Dutch, from Scheveningen." She laughed at him. "What do you think of my 'sch'?"

Like any Dutchman, DeKok knew that the "sch" sound, which is pronounced as a single letter, is just about impossible for a foreigner to pronounce properly.

"Very good," praised DeKok. He tossed her the panties and the bra. "Put something on, you'll catch a cold."

She caught the clothing.

"You're just like my grandfather," she griped. "He would always yell at me when he saw me naked."

"Perhaps he liked dressed Ingeborg better than naked Inge," smiled DeKok.

She let the words sink in. Then she gave him a tender look.

"You're not bad … for a cop."

DeKok accepted the compliment placidly. He watched as she put on the bra and pulled on the panties under the blanket. Then she stepped out of bed. She was beautiful, he observed, tall, slender with a feline grace. When she put on a blouse, he saw the puncture marks on her arm.

Their eyes crossed.

"How long have you been on heroin?"

"Two years."

"You started because of Igor?"

Inge shook her head as she put her long legs into a pair of black jeans.

"I was already a user before I knew Igor."

"Have you seen him? That is since you returned from Germany?"

"No."

"He's been asking for you."

"I heard that."

"Does he know you're here?" asked DeKok while he gestured around the room.

"Yes."

"How?"

She smiled sadly.

"Nothing stays a secret with Igor. I was back here less than an hour when he called me on the phone."

DeKok gave her a searching look.

"Do you know where he is?"

German Inge's comfort level suddenly changed. She took a cigarette from an open pack next to the bed and turned it around in her hand.

"I don't know where he is," she said hesitatingly. "I've never known much. Sometimes he comes over ... for a night." She pointed at the telephone. "Most of the time he just rings."

"When?"

Again the sad, tired smile.

"At night ... always at night ... to ask me how much I made."

"Last night?"

"What do you mean?"

Did Igor call you last night?"

"Yes."

"What time?"

"Half past one ... two o'clock ... thereabouts."

"When Izaak was here?"

She lit the cigarette from a lighter and took a long drag. She exhaled. Through the smoke she looked at the inspector with suspicion.

"You know that?"

DeKok nodded.

"I was outside. I saw Izaak come and leave."

"Why were you outside … watching?"

"I wanted to know if you had come back."

Inge shook her head.

"Please, spare me. You weren't there to see if I was back. I went to the station house myself. The missing person report had been cancelled for hours." She waved her cigarette around. "You were there to catch Igor, or you were following Izaak."

DeKok felt a hint of embarrassment. Inge had answered all his questions readily enough and she was not dumb. He should not have underestimated her by being untruthful.

"You're right, Inge," he said. "I was hoping to catch Igor and I was dumbfounded when you received Izaak Bildijk." He rubbed the back of his neck. "Is … eh, is Izaak one of your johns?"

"No."

"Not a client? I'm surprised. Then why was he here? What did he do?"

She stood up from the bed and walked away. She stopped a few yards away from DeKok. Her back was turned.

The inspector did not press her. He waited a while and then repeated his question in a friendly tone of voice.

"What did he do?"

"He waited."

"What for?"

"For Igor to phone."

DeKok could hardly hide his astonishment. He came out of his chair and walked over to the girl. His brain was working at full speed.

"Izaak talked to Igor?"

"Yes."

"What about?"

Suddenly she turned around. There were tears in her eyes.

"Ask Izaak," she answered.

"Izaak is dead," said DeKok bluntly.

Inge stiffened. Her eyes were big and frightened.

"Dead?" she whispered in a low tone.

DeKok nodded in confirmation.

"Somebody broke his skull." His tone was harsh and brutal.

For a moment it seemed as if the girl would faint. She swayed, but recovered herself. She hid her face in her hands.

"No ... NO ... NO!" she screamed.

Vledder entered the room. He was pale.

"What's happening," he asked.

DeKok shooed him away without an answer. He took Inge by the shoulders and shook her gently.

"What did Igor and Izaak talk about?"

She screamed again, louder.

"NO ... NO!!"

DeKok shook her more forcefully. Then he took her wrists and pulled her hands away from her face. He looked at her with a friendly face.

"It's important, Inge," he whispered. "Very important."

She was reduced to a quiet sobbing. DeKok took a clean handkerchief from his pocket and patted her teary face. Then he put his arms around her and guided her back to the bed. Gently he seated her. She leaned against him.

"You heard the conversation, didn't you?"

She nodded vaguely.

"Tell me."

"It was all about an inheritance ..."

"Yes."

"It was Izaak's inheritance. Igor was to get a share of it."

"When?"

The girl swallowed.

"As soon, as soon as ... as soon as Igor killed his rich aunt."

13

DeKok had tired feet. That is what he called the ailment. But it was more than just tired feet. The pain started in his toes, shot past his ankles, and settled in his calves. It felt like a thousand devils were poking his legs with little, red-hot pitchforks. He understood the pain was psychosomatic, but that did not make it any less real or debilitating. He knew what the pain meant. The investigation was going badly. He still had a feeling he'd lost his sense of direction. As ever, the solution seemed farther and farther away. His feet were reminding him. The maddening thing was no doctor had ever been able to diagnose a physical cause. Nothing DeKok did to alleviate the pain ever worked. As far as his body was concerned, the pain was simply not there. It was all in his mind.

His face contorted, he carefully lifted his legs and placed his feet gently on the edge of his desk. A sigh of temporary relief escaped him.

Vledder looked worried. He knew all about his partner's remarkable affliction and what it meant. Over the years the young man had suggested numerous remedies. By now he knew the only cure was a drastic change in the progress of whatever case they happened to be working on.

"You got it again?" Vledder asked sympathetically.

DeKok answered with a single nod, while he rubbed

his calves. It seemed to help a little, because after a while he leaned back with a sigh.

"I felt sorry for Inge," DeKok said after a long silence. "I liked her. It was too bad I had to treat her harshly. She was very upset. Once she finally calmed down she became fearful all over again. She is legitimately worried what Igor will do, if he finds out she talked to me."

"Knowing Igor," agreed Vledder, "she could very well be in danger."

DeKok nodded thoughtfully.

"I made her solemn promise that her statements would never be a part of any official report."

"Sometimes I can't comprehend you. You obtained the statement legally. It's evidence."

"It isn't evidence of murder."

" Igor *did* conspire with Izaak to murder Isolde Bildijk."

"First of all, I'm not so sure about the legality of it all. Have you forgotten how we gained entry? Besides, it's only hearsay and ... Izaak is dead."

"Igor is alive."

"But he did not kill Isolde Bildijk."

"You mean he hasn't accepted Izaak's invitation?"

"Exactly."

A stubborn look came over Vledder's face and he shook his head in disgust.

"But that's not what happened," he said angrily. "I told you, it's a mistake; the wrong person was killed. That's all. Believe me, the Bildijk niece and nephews are keen for the inheritance. That's the central core ... the motive for it all. You found out that Izaak was even prepared to give up a part of his inheritance in order to reach that goal ... he hired himself an executioner."

"Igor Stablinsky?"

"That's it," said Vledder. "That's all there's to it. But something went wrong. Igor Stablinsky made a mistake and killed the wrong person."

"Not too smart."

"How's that?"

DeKok spread his hands in an eloquent gesture.

"According to you, Izaak hired Igor. So, Izaak would have been the man to pay him, *after* the killing." DeKok shook his head. "No, Igor isn't that stupid."

Vledder looked flustered.

"You tell me. How, exactly did this mess happen?"

"If I knew that," sighed DeKok, "my feet wouldn't hurt anymore." He leaned back in his chair a little farther. "I do not believe there was a mistake. Not only did someone murder Izaak in cold blood, it was deliberate." He paused and leaned forward with a groan and rearranged his feet on the desk. "Too many things in the error theory don't add up. We can't lose track of the anomalies when we draw conclusions."

"Anomalies such as …"

"First there was no sign of forced entry. Next, Izaak pinned a note to the door, asking not to be disturbed for breakfast. But he didn't sleep in the bed and he was still dressed."

"Granted, but what does it mean?"

"The neat, tidy bed and the attire lead me to believe the murderer struck shortly after Izaak returned home. Bearing in mind there were no signs of a break-in, only two scenarios work. He either admitted the killer to his room, or the killer waited to ambush him inside the room." DeKok rubbed a finger along the side of his nose before he went on. "And another thing," he continued, "Izaak was not some old man nodding off in his chair. Quite the contrary, Izaak was still young, virile, and wide awake. If somebody had tried to enter his room surreptitiously, he would have noticed."

"So, the killer did appear suddenly." Vledder sounded skeptical.

"No."

"But Izaak was killed nevertheless."

"Yes. The killer, however, was somebody who did not frighten him. He trusted the individual, at least the extent he did not expect an attack."

"A member of the family!" exclaimed Vledder.

DeKok did not answer. Carefully he stood up and waddled to the peg where his coat was kept. Vledder stood up as well.

"Where are you going?"

DeKok turned half way.

"To Lowee ... maybe a cognac will relieve the pain in my feet."

DeKok ambled sedately through the Quarter. Despite the early hour, it was busy. The chilled wind and rain had temporarily let up. A mild spring sun coaxed people outside. But the sex cinemas were playing to full houses and the porno shops attracted a lot of window shoppers.

Vledder walked a few paces ahead. He was partly breaking a path for DeKok and partly struggling to match even DeKok's more leisurely pace.

In passing, DeKok lifted his hat for Aunt Mary, a semi-retired madam of a small brothel. He had known her for as long as he had been stationed at Warmoes Street. She's getting old, he thought. The dyed hair seemed to make her older. He thought sadly about the early days. Back in the day, Mary was the most gorgeous woman on the street. She was fiery, full of temperament. Nobody dreamt of calling her 'aunt.'

DeKok glanced at his own reflection in a shop window and grinned ruefully. The years had not passed him by without leaving their mark. He noted it with a resigned sort of acquiescence. It did not make him somber or sad. He accepted it. He had become more massive and more compact. Everything seemed to have sunk down to his hips. It was a long time since he had seen any hair on his head that was not gray. These were superficial changes; his heart was still strong. The desire to keep fighting crime his way had not abated at all.

Lowee greeted the two inspectors in his usual exuberant way. He quickly wiped his hands on his stained vest.

"Well, well," he chirped. "Good to see youse." He gave DeKok a keen look. His narrow ferret face gleamed with good will. "Everything honkeedoree?"

DeKok grinned.

"Your concern overwhelms me, Lowee. Sometimes you remind me of my mother."

The little barkeeper cocked his hat.

"Nah, but you gotta deal wit'lottsa nuts. They'll stick anyboddy inna ribs for a coupla bucks. Seem like they'se aroun' in … incre … allatime there's more of'em."

DeKok hoisted himself on a barstool.

"We will all have to learn to live with it. The times when a judge still considered a knife wielder as a dangerous individual are long since past." He grinned sadly. "Everybody is carrying a weapon these days."

Lowee nodded in agreement.

"Same recipe?"

Without waiting for an answer, he reached under the bar and produced a bottle of Napoleon cognac. With the other hand he lined up three large snifters. With a routine gesture he filled the glasses and replaced the bottle. He lifted one of the glasses.

"Proost ... to a better world."

DeKok winked.

"A world without crime, Lowee?"

The barkeeper grinned.

"Well, sorta," he said. "Lookit, DeKok, you gotta face it, no sin, no job."

"I have a house, a wife, a dog, and, since recently, a parakeet."

"And that gonna fill youse days?"

DeKok raised his head and pushed his chin forward.

"I could write my memoirs. It's the fashion nowadays, you know."

Lowee looked gleeful.

"You gonna write about me, too?"

"Certainly."

"Wadda ye gonna write about me then?"

"What do you think?"

Lowee's face became expressionless.

"You shoulda write about me as Holy Lowee ... the Saint ya know, witta ariool over ma head."

DeKok laughed heartily. He picked up his glass, rocked it carefully in his hand, and then let the golden liquid run down his throat.

"Ahh," he said with complete satisfaction.

Lowee put his glass back on the counter.

"You seen Crazy Chris?"

"Yes."

"And?"

DeKok took another sip of cognac.

"We found Igor's girl." He looked at Lowee. "But we haven't found Igor."

"He was here," said Lowee, making a vague gesture around the room.

"Who ... Igor?"

"Yessir."

"When?"

"Yestiday."

DeKok looked stunned.

"Why did you not warn me?" He swallowed. "You know how dangerous that guy is. Every hour he's on the loose, he ..." DeKok did not finish the sentence.

Lowee raised both arms. His face was a picture of innocence.

"Hey, I hadda full house, DeKok. Packed. I couldna just up and leave. I couldna gettat da phone. Too busy. Nobody to take over for me. Anyways, he was gone in no time. I give him da phone number, he takes a beer and go."

DeKok gave him a long, thoughtful look. He understood Lowee very well. There had been too many people around who could have overheard Lowee talking to DeKok on the phone. In all conscience he could not blame Lowee.

"A phone number?" Asked DeKok after a long pause.

"Yessir."

"What kind of phone number?"

Lowee separated the glasses and leaned confidentially across the bar, closer to DeKok.

"Yestiday mornin'," he whispered. "This guy comes in

here. A real toff. He axed me how he's gonna reach Igor. I says that's sorta hard, the cops is lookin' for 'em. He says never mind, I gotta talk to 'im and what were I gonna do about it? He gives me a hunnert bucks."

DeKok listened intently.

"Then what?"

Lowee shrugged his shoulders.

"I says to the guy it ain't easy, but I woulda look out for 'im. Then he gives me da card widda phone number. You tells Igor to call me, he says."

DeKok sighed.

"And you gave that number to Igor."

"Of course, small job for a hunnert bucks, ain't it? It waz just lucky datta shows up here da same day. He ain't here that much."

"Do you remember the number?"

Lowee gave DeKok a secretive smile.

"Yep. I done wrote it down. I thinks dadda would be nice for youse."

He turned to the back of the bar and retrieved a piece of paper from between some bottles. DeKok accepted it.

"Zero, twenty-nine, sixty-three," he read aloud. "Fifteen, seventy-four, eighty."

Vledder read over his shoulder.

"That's the area code for Oldkerk."

DeKok nodded slowly.

"Yes, and Izaak Bildijk's number."

14

From Lowee's bar they crossed Rear Fort Canal toward Old Church Square. Both Vledder and DeKok were lost in thought.

Vledder finally broke the silence.

"Igor's reputation as a crook who preys on elderly people must somehow have reached Izaak."

DeKok nodded.

"It wouldn't have been difficult for Izaak to get the word. Igor's arrest for the murder of Sam Lion and his subsequent escape have been in all the papers."

"I just don't understand how they established contact with each other."

"Once Izaak made contact, Igor undoubtedly directed Izaak to Inge's residence, figuring it would be a safe venue. The conspiracy was the easy part; it wouldn't have taken long to work out a plan."

"But that contact was already in place. Little Lowee gave Igor Izaak's number. So Igor must have called him to give him Inge's address."

DeKok shook his head.

"You don't have enough imagination. Just think. Izaak Bildijk spent most of his time at Happy Lake, with his aunt. Izaak could hardly give Lowee the number of his aunt. Izaak could not be certain to answer that phone when someone called. If you call Izaak's number, I bet you'll get an answering machine."

"Of course, Igor left a message. There never was any direct contact, until Izaak answered Inge's phone."

DeKok nodded wisely.

"Very good, you'll make a real police officer, someday."

For a while they walked on; Vledder in wounded silence.

On the corner of Narrow Church Alley and Warmoes Street, he stopped suddenly.

"You think that message is still on the answering machine?"

"Possibly. The Oldkerk police may have found it. This case is so confusing with overlapping territories, I don't know anymore who is doing what." DeKok sounded annoyed. "All because of those bedeviled geese," he added.

"But," replied Vledder, "maybe Igor said something we can use."

"Fine, go ahead and track down that answering machine. But let's stop by the station first, and find out if there's anything new."

"See, that's why we should have radios," protested Vledder. He knew it was a useless argument. DeKok still resisted the radio in the police car. Had always resisted the walkie-talkies that had been issued. Every police officer in Holland now had the latest technology, a very compact, more powerful new radio. To Vledder's dismay, DeKok was the last hold out. "If they want me," was DeKok's catch phrase, "they can find me."

Not surprisingly therefore, DeKok ignored Vledder's protest and led the way to the station house.

As soon as they entered, Meindert Post hailed them.

"Where have you guys been?" he yelled. "I know DeKok can't be bothered with a radio, but I thought better of you," he added, pointing an accusing finger at Vledder.

DeKok did not apologize.

"A cop has to go out. As an old fisherman you should know that. Nobody catches fish on land."

Meindert Post ignored the remark and pointed to the ceiling.

"There's a woman waiting for you. She refuses to leave. She insists on speaking with you. It's very important, she said." Post grimaced and then added: "She's afraid she'll be murdered."

Vledder and DeKok climbed the staircase with the worn marble steps. A relatively young woman was waiting for them on the bench across from the detective room. As soon as she saw the inspectors, she rose and approached.

"Mrs. Isolde Bildijk has introduced us," she said. "Do you remember me, Irmgard Miller?"

DeKok lifted his hat and made a courteous bow.

"The charming mother of three charming children."

"An inexhaustible source of worry," she smiled.

DeKok led the way to the detective room and held the chair next to his desk for her. Meanwhile he studied her closely. At Happy Lake she had seemed mousy and nondescript, but there was a subtle change. She wore a tweed suit with a skirt that came to just below the knee. Her blonde hair curled in luxurious tresses around a clear-skinned face that was free of make-up. She crossed her legs and unbuttoned her coat. If he had not known better, DeKok would never have guessed that she was the mother of three children.

Her figure was superb. She looked at the inspector with bright green eyes that did not hide underlying worry.

"Strange things are happening at Happy Lake," she began.

Despite himself, DeKok grinned suddenly.

"How can you say that?" he asked mockingly.

She ignored the remark.

"The poisoned geese ... the death of the gardener ... the murder of my brother Izaak. I'm afraid. This morning, shortly after breakfast, my husband left on business. I don't want to desert Aunt Isolde, but I'm afraid to stay at the house at night."

DeKok nodded in agreement.

"What does your husband do for a living?"

"He's in textiles."

"And business is good?"

"Why do you ask?"

"It's well known," shrugged DeKok, "that the textile business in the Netherlands is not very prosperous at the moment. In some countries ..."

Irmgard interrupted.

"We're doing very well," she said sharply.

DeKok rubbed his chin thoughtfully.

"So, you're not exactly desperate for your inheritance?"

Irmgard's eyes spat fire.

"What are you driving at?" she asked, agitated. "When the gardener died, my husband wasn't even in town and when Izaak was killed, my husband was in bed with me."

"You're sure of that?"

Irmgard's attempt to control her temper was transparent. She took a deep breath before she answered.

"Yes," she said, calmer. "I'm sure. I'm a very light sleeper and I would have noticed if he had gotten up."

DeKok smiled an ironic smile.

"As a witness … a loving wife is not much value as a witness."

A brief look of despair appeared in her lovely green eyes. She shook her head, as if to clear it.

"I'm telling you what I know," said Irmgard with an emphasis she underscored with a definitive gesture. "My husband has nothing to do with what happened at Happy Lake."

"Who, then?"

She pointed at DeKok.

"That's your concern and, I might add, your responsibility."

DeKok sighed and nodded to himself. He paused for a while and then resumed his questioning.

"Did you hear Izaak come home, last night?"

"No," said Irmgard, shaking her head. "I told you I'm a light sleeper. I've tried all day to remember, but Izaak must have been careful to make no noise. If he had, I would undoubtedly have heard it."

"Any other noises?"

"No."

"Where's your bedroom?"

"Downstairs, next to Aunt Isolde."

"And does it have a window that looks out over the garden?"

"Indeed."

"No French doors, or any other kind of doors to the outside?"

Irmgard shook her head.

"Izaak's room is the only room with doors to the outside. When Uncle Iwert was still alive, it was their room, his and Aunt Isolde's."

"I see," said DeKok. "And the children?"

Irmgard Miller pointed at the ceiling.

"They sleep upstairs, on the second floor."

"Together?"

"No, each of them has a room."

"Even little Penny?"

Irmgard did not answer at once. She gave the inspector a long, searching look. A suspicious light came in her eyes.

"Have you ever talked to her?"

"Oh, yes," confirmed DeKok. "A very interesting conversation."

Irmgard reacted emphatically.

"Penny's a liar," she said, as if trying to convince herself, as well as DeKok. "That child is always full of fantasies, silly nonsense. What kind of fairy tale did she tell you?"

DeKok shook his head. A smile curled his lips.

"It was certainly no childish fantasy. In any event, Penny and I made a solemn promise not to discuss it with anyone else."

"That's ridiculous, I'm her mother."

DeKok raised his hands in defense.

"That's still no reason for me to break a promise."

Irmgard leaned forward.

"She's lying," she almost hissed.

DeKok made a nonchalant gesture.

"I presume you draw your conclusions based on personal experience with your daughter. My experiences indicate the opposite."

Irmgard Miller gripped her head as if at wit's end.

"But it is a lie," she exclaimed.

"What?"

"Aunt Isolde cannot walk."

Vledder looked a question at DeKok after Irmgard had left.

"Does that mean that Penny has seen her invalid aunt walk about and told her mother?"

"Yes," agreed DeKok. "And the mother was afraid that Penny had told me the same."

Vledder grinned as he finished some final entries on his computer.

"It was very amusing to listen to the two of you," said Vledder after he had put the computer on stand-by. "You were thinking of unrelated matters. You had in mind the escapades of Izaak and a stick, while she was busy denying Isolde's mobility."

DeKok also smiled as he gazed thoughtfully into the distance.

"Still," he said after a long pause, "the little girl kept her word. Apparently she did not tell her mother about seeing Izaak in the garden." He paused again, a serious look on his face. "However, Irmgard's defensive tone makes me believe her Aunt Isolde *is* mobile. Her ability to walk means we have a completely new dimension to consider in this case."

"I don't agree," said Vledder. "It does not change the facts. Isolde is not a participant. She's merely a prospective victim."

"Ah ... but whose victim?"

Vledder gesticulated vehemently, angrily.

"Who knows ... niece Irmgard, nephew Ivo, maybe both. Anyway Irmgard's fear of being murdered isn't credible, either. She doesn't seem too concerned about leaving Happy Lake ... that is, not before this dirty business is finished. We have only to wait for that."

"Isolde's obituary?"

"Exactly."

"Maybe you're right," shrugged DeKok.

"Of course I'm right," asserted Vledder. "Someone thinks we are so ignorant as to believe all this is the work of Igor Stablinsky."

"Who's only guilty of indirectly having supplied the method; he lent them his m. o.?"

"Right on, that's exactly the way it fits together."

"Maybe, but I'm not satisfied we know all the facts. If we don't get some positive results soon, we'll have to call all the jurisdictions together. We'll need Warmoes Street, Oldkerk, and the Twenty-third. By the way, how come we never heard anything more about that missing forensic team? We may even have to involve Bussum. I've not completely forgotten Uncle Immanuel, either. It's a mess ... too many cooks spoil the broth, you know." He walked over to the peg to get his coat, then he added: "I wonder if geese make a good soup." Then he turned to Vledder. "Are you coming?" he asked.

"Where?"

"Oldkerk."

"Oldkerk?"

"Yes, I want to see the late Izaak Bildijk's house."

Vledder parked the car on the even numbered side of Higher End, as Izaak's street was named. The inspectors exited the car and crossed the street.

"Do you have keys to the house?" asked DeKok.

"Yes," answered Vledder, noting that DeKok replaced his illegal instrument in his pocket. "There was a key ring in Izaak's coat. I lifted it."

"Found anything else?"

"A wallet with some money and a pocket agenda. I seems Izaak may have been homosexual. That is, I found the names and addresses of a few homosexual prostitutes in the agenda. But that was all. Anyway, I did not have the time to go over it in any detail. You'll have to do that later, or tomorrow. I've got an autopsy."

DeKok grinned maliciously.

"Izaak Bildijk will be an easy job for Dr. Rusteloos. He only has to copy the previous reports."

Vledder shook his head.

"He'll never do that. Every corpse gets the full treatment. He's much too conscientious." He pointed as they approached the door of Izaak's house. "What about the answering machine ... shall we just confiscate it and take it to Amsterdam for further study?"

DeKok nodded agreement.

They halted in front of number one hundred fifteen. It was an old brownstone from the middle of the previous century, with green shutters in front of the windows. The front door was recessed. Vledder took Izaak's key ring from his pocket and selected a key. As he tried to put it in the keyhole, the door moved. He looked at DeKok.

"The door isn't locked."

"Evidently," answered DeKok. He leaned forward, but could not detect signs of a forcible entry. He pressed his elbow against the door and opened it wider. He stepped inside, with Vledder right behind him.

From a small foyer with a staircase leading up, they reached a main corridor with oaken wainscoting. The house smelled damp and stuffy.

To the right, almost at the end of the corridor, a door

was ajar. Silently DeKok passed the door and then turned. With a sudden movement he crashed open the door.

A man could be seen in the room. He stood in front of a massive oaken chest. His face was pale and his puffy hands trembled.

DeKok sneered tauntingly.

"Well, well," he said, "as I live and breathe ... Nephew Ivo! How is it we just keep running into you?"

15

DeKok approached Bildijk and pushed him roughly into a nearby easy chair. Then he took a seat opposite the flustered man.

"You *do* have a special knack of being the first on the scene of a crime, wouldn't you agree? You also seem to have a talent for scavenging, for searching the belongings of the recently deceased." His tone was sarcastic. "Perhaps you would enlighten us as to how you got in here and why?"

Ivo Bildijk did not answer at once. He clearly paused to gather himself and regain his composure. Slowly the color came back in his cheeks. With a still shaking hand he put his hand in a pocket and produced a key. With an innocent gesture he raised the key to eye level.

"Aunt Isolde remembered there's a woman who comes and cleans for Izaak once a week. She had a key and I borrowed it."

"That sounds believable," growled DeKok.

Ivo Bildijk gave him a wan smile.

"You can check it out," he said. "Very simple. We'll return the key together." He took a deep breath "And as far as your second question is concerned ... why am I here? That is your own fault."

"Me?" asked DeKok, apparently genuinely flabbergasted.

"Yes, despite our producing the threatening letters with

their postmarks, you did not arrest our gardener. Considering your reputation as a great detective, it made Aunt Isolde and I think twice. During our latest conversation you felt it was a remarkable coincidence Izaak lived in Oldkerk. We know Oldkerk was the postmark on the letters. Well, it was enough for Aunt Isolde to order me to investigate further in Izaak's house. She wants me to look for stationery, envelopes. You understand … for my aunt, as well as for me … it would be a relief if we knew where those letters originated."

DeKok's annoyance with the slippery, greasy man in the chair across from him was getting worse. It threatened to get the better of him. The man seemed to have a pat answer for every situation. Despite flawless preparation and smooth delivery, he failed to convince DeKok. The senior inspector found it difficult to decide what he disliked more, the man himself, or the way in which he delivered his lines in his unctuous voice.

"Aunt Isolde says: Go to the house of the old gardener, and you go. Aunt Isolde says: Go to the house of dead Izaak, and you go." DeKok gesticulated wildly, partly from anger and partly from frustration. "What are you—a lackey to the self-styled duchess of Happy Lake?"

Bildijk came half out of his chair. He had a change of heart, letting himself fall back into the deep cushions.

"I forbid you," said Ivo evenly, "to speak in that manner about my aunt."

"You're that close to her, are you?"

Ivo Bildijk's face assumed a sad expression.

"I'm her oldest nephew," he said resignedly. "Over the years we have established a sort of mutual trust. I have become her confidant. It's no more than reasonable for her to discuss certain things with me. It is also reasonable for me to

take care of certain matters for her. After all she is an invalid.
I ... I fail to see how that could possibly offend you."

DeKok took a deep breath.

"I'm looking for a possible motive for two horrible murders ... murders that happened in your immediate surroundings. One way or the other these ugly events are connected
to you." He paused for effect. "Mr. Bildijk, for once give me
a straight forward answer: Are you afraid of being killed?"

Ivo was shaken. For the first time he showed some weak-
ness, a breach in the wall of his self-satisfied eloquence. He
turned pale but kept silent."

DeKok looked his most intimidating.

"I repeat: Are you afraid of being murdered?"

Ivo sank deeper into the chair and with a quick gesture
wiped his brow.

"Yes," he said, barely audible.

"Why?"

"I'm one of the heirs."

DeKok leaned forward and held Ivo's eyes with his own.
"Who?"

Bildijk swallowed, flicked a tongue across dry lips and
tried unsuccessfully to break DeKok's stare. DeKok waited.

"Ask Irmgard," whispered Ivo Bildijk finally.

Vledder was in a good mood. He took the corners with all
the elan the old VW could muster. He whistled a song with
a smile on his face. He accompanied himself by tapping the
fingers of one hand on the steering wheel.

DeKok watched him glumly.

"What's got into you? You're sure you're still playing
with a full deck?"

Vledder stopped whistling and turned briefly toward DeKok with a satisfied smile on his face.

"I was right," crowed Vledder.

"That'll be a first," said DeKok sadly.

The young inspector laughed out loud.

"I told you ... everything is tied to Isolde's inheritance. Just think, there were three heirs: Ivo, Izaak, and Irmgard. And now Izaak is dead."

"And that leaves two," mocked DeKok.

"Yes, and both are afraid of being murdered."

"By whom?"

"By the other," said Vledder triumphantly.

"Aha," said DeKok, "then you've changed your opinion. Izaak's murder was no mistake, but intentionally committed by Ivo, Irmgard, or both."

"Yes."

"You think brother and sister are now engaged in a game of "Last Man Standing." Each wants to murder the other – the last one takes it all."

Vledder playfully slapped his partner's knee.

"That's the way it is," he said elatedly.

DeKok slid further down in the seat and pulled his hat down on his forehead.

"You overlooked one tiny detail."

"And what's that?" Vledder wanted to know.

"The murder of old Willem still doesn't fit. In the elimination contest for riches, it is just as we said, a senseless waste."

"No, not senseless. If Isolde hasn't altered her husband's testament ... and there is no basis to believe otherwise ... the gardener would be richly rewarded. Weren't those Willem's own words?"

"How would the other heirs know that?"

"Not impossible," shrugged Vledder. "They may have seen the testament. Then there's the possibility old Willem told them himself. He told you."

DeKok made a vague gesture.

"I don't think 'richly rewarded' means a great deal. It's probably some sort of settlement in kind or a monetary settlement, but hardly comparable to the shares of the other heirs."

"For someone who is bound and determined, it could still be a motive."

DeKok growled something inaudible, but did not react in any other way.

The road from Oldkerk led past the Bildijk mansion. Vledder pointed at the closed gate.

"Should we take another look?"

DeKok slid even further down in the seat and shook his head.

"If Irmgard went home and cracked Isolde's head, we'll get a news flash soon enough. He sounded completely disinterested.

"Then where do you want to go?," asked Vledder.

DeKok looked at his watch. It was almost seven o'clock.

"First let's have a bite to eat, something Indonesian, I think. Then how about we return to Leiden Side Street. I've a sudden urge to see Inge ... for another conversation, of course."

Vledder looked at his partner.

"On one condition ... I don't have to stay in the kitchen again."

"Any other wishes?"

Vledder nodded.

"This time we'll just ring the doorbell."

"My, we're getting to be demanding."

"It's also the first time I'm right," laughed Vledder.

German Inge looked surprised when she answered the door.

"Are you here again? I was just about to leave. At this time it's easy to pick up an early customer. I call it overtime."

"Overtime?" asked Vledder.

She gave Vledder a quick look, but smiled naughtily at DeKok.

"Men tell their wives they have to work overtime. Can they help it if it is more tempting to take a little trip in the car with me."

"With the necessary stop," commented DeKok.

"I'm in 'the life'—it's how I make a little extra," she shrugged. Then she looked him up and down. "Did you guys stop by for business advice or just girl talk?"

"Neither," said DeKok, "I could not help wondering whether Igor phoned to tell you he bashed in the wrong skull last night."

Inge took a step back and they moved into her room. Inge sat down on the bed and the inspectors found chairs.

"Igor didn't call," said Inge. She produced a cigarette paper and some tobacco. Slowly she started to roll a cigarette. "I told you before," she continued, her attention on the cigarette she was forming in her hands. "Igor only calls at night. He's nocturnal. He's afraid of the daylight."

DeKok nodded.

"A nocturnal predator," he said.

"Yes," she said, "I called him a night owl once. He became angry. He gets angry easily."

She had finished the cigarette and rummaged on the bedside table for some matches.

"Igor's parents—are they still alive?," asked DeKok as she lit the cigarette. Both inspectors were immediately aware she was not smoking tobacco. Neither mentioned it. Drug trafficking is illegal in the Netherlands, not drug use. "Does he have any brothers ... sisters?" continued DeKok. "Have you ever discussed his family?" he added.

Inge took a deep drag before she answered.

"Something always made me reluctant to raise the subject of family," she said.

DeKok told her what he knew about Igor.

"Igor is a Pole. He was born in Gdansk, according to his Dutch passport. He's a fairly recent émigré, who became a Dutch citizen at twenty-three." DeKok rubbed the back of his neck. "The records don't say much more. We investigated on our own. The family records in Gdansk were destroyed in a bombardment. We can only speculate whether they were destroyed for political reasons."

"I didn't know that."

"What language do you speak when you are together?"

"Dutch."

DeKok leaned forward.

"Is Igor ..." he began hesitantly, "Is Igor sexually dependent on you?"

"You mean, am I his addiction?"

"Something like that, yes."

"No," she said softly, "It's more the other way around. There's something mysterious, something wild about Igor. Maybe untouchable wildness attracts a woman. I can't put it in words, but there's a certain charm about Igor, a charm that does something to me."

DeKok listened carefully to the tone and the passion of her words.

"What do you really know about him?"

"Nothing ... not much," she admitted.

"Are you aware he's suspected of the murders of at least two elderly people?"

Inge nodded slowly, taking another drag from her cigarette.

"Yes, I've heard something like that."

"And?"

The young woman looked at DeKok and there was something in her glance that warned DeKok.

"What ... and?" she almost screamed. "Why should I care if Igor killed a few old people? He'd leave me flat, rather than stop doing whatever he does." She snorted contemptuously. "But do you really think I think about *that* when we're together?"

DeKok sighed.

"It's obvious I will not get much cooperation from you."

"To catch Igor?" she sneered.

"For instance."

German Inge shook her head decisively.

"Never," she said with bowed head. "I know," she continued, softer, more gently, "he's going to be arrested one of these days. Nothing lasts forever. It is easy to imagine he'll go to prison ... for longer than any woman could wait for him." She looked resigned as she met DeKok's eyes. "If or when that happens, I'll go back to Hanover. Perhaps I'll meet another man ... a man like Igor."

16

_____

Vledder still had a smile on and DeKok still looked stern, as they drove back to the station house. The young inspector could not contain himself any longer. He took a perverse, malicious pleasure in DeKok's chagrin.

"This case is not going at all well, DeKok," said Vledder. "It just isn't your day. Inge will not cooperate."

"Too bad," answered DeKok sedately. He seemed unruffled.

"Ha!"

"Yes," continued DeKok as if Vledder had not interrupted at all. "She's actually the only link we have to Igor, at this moment. We can hardly keep her under twenty-four hour surveillance in the hope Igor will show up … though it may have to come to that."

"Ha," said Vledder again. "In that case you better ask the commissaris to break open another crate of cops. You know we don't have the personnel."

"What makes me saddest of all … what really bothers me, is her motive for refusing to help us … her philosophy." DeKok was just continuing a monologue. He probably had not heard Vledder at all. But Vledder had heard DeKok and wanted to know more.

"What do you mean?"

"Narcissism … just narcissism. Wild, sensual Igor sometimes gives me a few hours of pleasure. No matter if he brutalizes and murders the elderly for profit ... I'm not interested."

"What can you do ... she loves the guy."

"I did not hear the word love mentioned even once."

Vledder shook his head.

"You're behind the times. Your ideas and opinions are old fashioned. What do you expect from a girl like that ... morals, ethics?"

"Humanity."

"Humanity ... from a whore?"

"Correct ... from a whore."

Vledder could not agree.

"When she finds another ..." he exclaimed full of emotion, "another guy who'll give her the same sort of pleasure ... she'll drop Igor like a hot potato." He grinned. "Your trouble, DeKok, is that you don't belong in this time period. You're descended from a generation of romantics ... a dying breed. You're probably the only remnant of the Age of Chivalry."

Suddenly DeKok sat up straight.

"Descended ... descend ... generation ... descendant ... offspring ... family," he said to himself.

He looked through the windshield.

"Where are you going," he demanded.

"To the station, of course," answered Vledder. "It's late, I want to go home."

"Nix on that," said DeKok in a tone that did not allow any argument. "We're going to Bussum. I promised myself an interview with Uncle Immanuel.

It was around midnight when they entered the town of Bussum. DeKok looked at his watch. He was shocked by the time.

"It's really too late to visit this frail old man," he winced.

"Well you just had to come here," growled Vledder. "Uncle Immanuel has no doubt gone to his bed."

They parked the car on Bredius Way, exited, and locked the car. DeKok pointed at a villa across the way.

"That is a well kept, free-standing single family dwelling, near a luscious lake, surrounded by a prize winning garden. Includes all appliances, large two-car garage, central heating, and alarm system."

"Where did that come from," asked Vledder, nonplussed.

"From an advertisement in the paper," said DeKok complacently. "That villa is for sale."

"Uncle Immanuel is selling?"

"Apparently," confirmed DeKok, "I checked it out with the realtor. Immanuel is selling his house. Perhaps he doesn't feel safe in Bussum any longer."

Vledder frowned.

"You may be right," he admitted. "As soon as Aunt Isolde has been removed, it may very well be his turn."

They walked toward the house. An entire side of the house was covered in ivy. The impenetrable black vines provided a gothic look, especially after dark. There was a large bay window to one side and a large double door with a small, barred window in each panel. A brass knocker in the shape of a lion's head was mounted on the right leaf of the double door. More like a gargoyle's face than a lion's, it lent itself to the gothic mood.

DeKok looked at the surroundings. The dense vegetation around the house gave him a claustrophobic feeling. He shook his head in disapproval.

"This may be a prize-winning garden," he murmured, "but there are too many shadows where an intruder could hide."

He took the knocker in his hand, hammering three times rather hard. The mahogany door acted as a perfect sounding board. They could hear the reverberations from inside.

In a few minutes the two inspectors suddenly stood in the harsh light from a number of spotlights. The little, barred window opened. Behind the bars, in the reflected light from the spotlights, they could see a wizened face. There was a look of suspicion and astonishment in the old gentleman's eyes.

DeKok politely took off his hat and showed his full face.

"My name is DeKok," he said with a friendly smile. "DeKok with kay-oh-kay." He moved aside. "And this is my colleague Vledder. We are Police Inspectors."

The old man's eyes narrowed.

"Are you the ones in charge of that mess at Happy Lake?"

DeKok nodded.

"Yes, we are. And you are Immanuel Bildijk?"

"Indeed."

The face disappeared and the small window closed. A few moments later the right half of the double door opened. The old man beckoned.

"Come in quickly, so I can lock the door again. Everything changes—all sorts of scum in the streets these days." He laughed loud and chirping. "But why am I telling you? You have a working knowledge."

Shuffling, in a robe and a pair of too large leather slippers, he led the way to a comfortably furnished den. The room was lit with the muted light from a number of lamps with green glass shades. With a courtly gesture the old man waved toward a circle of deep, comfortable leather chairs.

"Please, sit down, gentlemen. Adele, my housekeeper has already gone to bed, She suffers from migraines. I can only offer you a glass of Burgundy." His voice was high and rasped just a little. "That's a good habit ... a glass of good Burgundy before retiring. The British aristocracy has done it for generations ... but they call it *claret* ... never knew why."

He took a finely cut decanter from a side table and filled three glasses. He took one of them, urging Vledder and DeKok to do the same. He raised his glass to them.

"Proost ... to my and your health."

DeKok took a sip and then a large swallow. The wine was indeed excellent. From behind his glass he looked at the old man.

"That's the reason for our visit ... generations."

Uncle Immanuel nodded, as in confirmation of an unspoken revelation.

"I had expected you sooner."

DeKok carefully placed his glass on a small side table next to his chair.

"We planned to come sooner, but the death of your nephew Izaak prevented it."

The old man looked surprised.

"What ... Izaak is dead, too?"

"Murdered."

Immanuel shook his head sadly.

"One should never turn one's back on a Bildijk."

Both Vledder and DeKok sat up straight.

"Is the murderer a Bildijk?," asked DeKok.

The old man smiled.

"I'm almost sure of it." There was resignation in his voice. "They all have a flaw ... the Bildijk flaw."

"And that is?"

"Intellectually gifted and ... larcenous."

"A dangerous combination."

"Unfortunately it works like a curse for some; the clever, ruthless ones have a fatal flaw."

"How so?"

Immanuel sighed deeply and placed his glass on the table next to his own chair.

"They have no scruples. They keep going until they destroy themselves."

DeKok favored him with an admiring look.

"But you're still around ... exceptional ... and at a ripe age. And you're in no way as demented as your nephew Ivo would have us believe."

The old man scratched behind his ear; thought about his answer.

"Perhaps..." he began, "Or else I've been able to hide the Bildijk flaw a little better. Anyway I'm more intellectual than criminal. Besides, my name is Immanuel, which means 'God with you.'"

DeKok nodded with a serious, reflective face.

"God with you," he repeated. "Yes, there is something in a name. He paused in thought. "All Christian names," he continued, "in the Bildijk family start with the letter 'I' ... isn't that a bit unusual?"

The old man laughed.

"My father was an exceptional kind of man. He gathered a fortune in a very short time, which allowed him to buy the Happy Lake estate. It's much more than just the house and garden, you know. Once he settled down, he had four sons. Because he fancied the 'I' was the most pleasing sound in the alphabet, he called his sons Ignatius, Iwert, Immanuel, and Ilja."

"But only Immanuel is left."

"Yes, Ignatius inherited Happy Lake with all that was attached. He was the eldest so it was his right. Iwert and I went into business … trading mostly. I wound up in the diamond trade. I knew little about it, especially in the beginning. But I had an intuition for picking the right people … people who *did* know."

"And what about Ilja?"

"He was my youngest brother. He died first. The children, Ivo, Izaak, and Irmgard, are his."

"He perpetuated the 'I' tradition."

A smile of remembrance came over the old man's face.

"Ilja resembled my father in many ways. But he never managed to prosper. He died relatively poor."

DeKok picked up his glass and drained it. Vledder momentarily put down his notebook and followed suit. DeKok looked thoughtfully at Vledder and waited until he had picked up his notebook and pen again, before he asked the next question. The pause had been unobtrusive.

"Your other brothers …" resumed DeKok, "did they have any children?"

Immanuel Bildijk seemed surprised at the question.

"Ignatius had one daughter … Isolde."

DeKok's eyebrows briefly performed their incredible gymnastics. Immanuel looked for a moment as if he could not believe his own eyes, Vledder never noticed. Pen poised, he waited for the next question.

"Isolde?" asked DeKok.

"Yes, another 'I,'" grinned the old man.

"Would that be …" hesitated DeKok. "Would that be the same Isolde who now lives at Happy Lake, *that* Isolde?"

"Yes."

"But I understood she was married to Iwert … how's that possible? I mean … Iwert was her father's brother … he was her uncle … a real uncle."

Uncle Immanuel rose from his chair.

"Come, let me pour you another glass." He grinned shyly. "I promise you, it's going to be interesting."

DeKok could not contain his impatience.

"Surely Isolde can't have married her blood uncle."

The old man waved the question away. He poured from the decanter until all three glasses were full again. Then he sank back down in his chair.

"Not so hasty, young man," he said crabbily. Vledder suppressed a giggle at hearing DeKok being addressed as a *young* man. Immanuel took a good swallow of his wine and placed the glass on the tray, next to the decanter.

"Isolde …" he finally said, "was a, how shall I put it … a wild girl. As a young woman she was beautiful, wild, fiery, and passionate. She could not be tamed … restrained. Her behavior brought Ignatius and her mother to grief. She was only sixteen when she had … eh, relations with unsavory men. She stayed out all night and the family's reputation was shredded to bits by the neighbors. Holland wasn't always as tolerant as today. In those days the people had a strict sense of propriety. Circumspect behavior was absolutely expected."

He paused in reflection, but this time DeKok did not urge him on. He patiently waited for the rest of the story.

"When she was about eighteen," resumed Immanuel, "Isolde suddenly showed up with a violinist … a nondescript, vague sort of man, who traveled across Europe with his violin. The next day, she and the violinist disappeared. My brother Ignatius did everything possible to get her back. He asked the police for help and spent a small fortune on private detectives. It was all to no avail. She seemed to have gone up in smoke."

Uncle Immanuel took a sip of his wine. After he put the glass down again, his voice was a little less raspy.

"But about five years later," he continued, "Isolde suddenly re-emerged, alone. She refused to talk about the five years she had been gone. 'That's all over,' she would say. As her parents were dead, she soon claimed Happy Lake for herself. That's when I became involved. I was incensed at the time. I made it crystal clear she was in no way entitled to remove Iwert from his rightful inheritance. For years they lived together on the estate, Iwert and Isolde. They lived separate lives, each on their own floor. Still they were together in that large mansion. People thought it strange. Isolde was still a very attractive woman, so the inevitable rumors started to circulate. Although people did not know they were related, most knew the two were not married. In those days it was just never done. To quell all the rumors, Iwert and Isolde eventually married."

"Surely they had to have dispensation from the Crown."

Uncle Immanuel made a sad gesture.

"I don't know." He shrugged his shoulders. "Anyway, the marriage did not last long … about three years. Then Iwert died. Isolde has lived there alone since his death."

"But with old Willem, until recently."

"Indeed, Iwert is the one who hired him."

DeKok held his head at an angle.

"Do Ilja's children know the background of their aunt?"

Immanuel reached for his glass and shook his head.

"Of course not. It would only burden them. Anyway what's the use of raking up the past? We've always remained silent about Isolde's lascivious behavior."

The men fell silent. DeKok sipped from his wine. The luscious bouquet seemed to sharpen his thought processes. He gestured around the comfortable den.

"You want to leave here?"

"Yes," answered Immanuel. His voice was melancholy. "Several times now, I've seen Isolde's whelp slink around the house. It's not that I'm afraid to confront him. But I certainly wouldn't turn my back on him, not even for a moment. I'd be an easy target."

"Isolde's whelp?" asked DeKok. "What do you mean … a son?"

The old man waved a trembling arm.

"Igor."

17

DeKok closed his eyes for a moment, as he processed the shattering news. With a resolute gesture he lifted his glass and drained it in one long swallow. Then he stood up and with a reassuring gesture, placed both hands on the old man's shoulders.

"Wait before you sell the house," he said urgently. "I'd encourage you to delay any decision, if only for a few days. You wouldn't want to live only with regrets. Old trees don't transplant easily." He gave Immanuel an encouraging grin. "Take care of yourself and don't let anybody inside ... even your nearest and dearest." He looked deep into the old man's eyes. "Now let us out quickly," he added.

Creaking, Uncle Immanuel stood up. He indicated the decanter. "There's plenty of Burgundy left." It sounded like a subdued protest.

DeKok shook his head.

"Not this time ... we'll be back one of these days."

As soon as the heavy door was closed and locked behind them, DeKok walked quickly to the old VW. Vledder followed a bit slower, deep in thought. DeKok urged him on.

"Come on," he urged his harried junior. "How much speed can you get from this wreck?"

"Depends what you need," answered Vledder, obviously confused by DeKok's haste and urgency.

DeKok pointed at the car.

"I need speed," barked DeKok. "To Happy Lake ... and don't spare this old war horse."

The car roared through the night. The chassis groaned and the engine whined in protest. A number of unidentifiable parts rattled. Vledder held the steering wheel solidly in both hands. Apparently the poor old car hadn't had a front-end alignment in recent memory. His glance roamed constantly between the road, the dashboard, both mirrors, and the rest of the late-night traffic. Despite flooring the VW, other vehicles easily overtook the hard-working vehicle.

Finally Vledder decided that the car would probably hold together for a while and he relaxed just a little. He still had to shout to be heard over the surrounding noise.

"Igor is Isolde's son?" he questioned. "It's incredible."

"Hindsight is twenty-twenty," DeKok roared back. "I can't believe I've been that stupid. I noticed the likeness between Isolde and Igor during my very first meetings. I just ignored it. When her name wasn't listed with those of Igor's victims, but separately, it should have rung a bell."

"I don't think it's Iwert's child," said Vledder, not as loud, but still loud enough to overcome the peripheral noise. "Willem said they had no children."

"The father must be the itinerant musician. Remember when Immanuel told us Isolde was missing for five years? He mentioned her having roamed Europe with this foreign violinist."

"So, *his* name must have also been Stablinsky."

"Yes, and it raises the possibility Isolde and Stablinsky were married."

"Well, had Isolde been unmarried at the time of Igor's birth, the child would have received his mother's last name. That's what happens in Holland and it's also usual in most other European countries."

"So Igor can inherit?"

"Certainly, if he's a lawful child."

For a moment it looked as if Vledder would lose control of the speeding vehicle. Quickly he regained control.

"If Igor can inherit ..." he yelled after a long pause, "what inheritance would there be for Ivo and Irmgard? Is it all the same inheritance?"

"If it's true."

"What's true?"

DeKok shook his head while he grabbed the ceiling strap. The car was leaning in the long curve of a ramp.

"What's true?" repeated Vledder after he had safely regained the new roadway.

"I'm not so sure Irmgard and Ivo are after the inheritance."

"Then it must have just been Izaak. We have evidence. He already hired a killer."

"Yes, Igor Stablinsky."

At the volume DeKok was using, the name sounded like a curse.

"Too many questions," yelled Vledder. "After five years Isolde came back alone, and she moved into Happy Lake. Where was the child? When did he surface? How? And what happened to Igor's father?"

DeKok did not answer. He agreed with Vledder, there were too many questions. Irritated, he looked aside.

"Can't you go faster?" yelled DeKok.

Vledder kept all his attention focused on the road; they were getting into a more densely populated area.

"What's the matter? You have a death wish?" snarled Vledder.

DeKok ran ahead.

The gate was half open, but he did not allow himself time to wait for it to fully open, so the car could pass. He sprinted down the gravel path. A sickly odor reached his nostrils. Out of the corner of one eye he saw that the heap of dead geese still had not been removed. He was too focused on his goal to get angry about it. He ran up to the mansion and climbed the steps at almost the same speed. He banged with a full fist on the door. Vledder breathed down his neck.

"There is a door bell," observed Vledder.

DeKok did not hear him. Without let-up he banged on the door with both fists. Lights came on in the house. It took almost another minute before the door opened. Irmgard appeared in the door opening ... a pale, frightened face above a red peignoir.

"DeKok!" she said, distressed.

DeKok passed her by. Then he turned back.

"Where's Ivo?"

Irmgard pointed hesitantly at a door.

"In his room ... I think."

DeKok ran to the indicated door and threw it open.

On the doorstep he stopped.

Ivo Bildijk's corpse leaned sideways in a deep, comfortable easy chair.

DeKok came closer and looked at the corpse. From just below the hairline of the slicked-down blond hair, a line of coagulated blood ran down next to his left ear. A small puddle of blood had formed on the flowery carpet. Ivo's clear blue eyes were wide open. They looked larger than in life and frightened, as if trying to understand what had happened. His killer had struck a single, powerful blow from the back. Again the victim had been unaware of the murderer's approach.

Behind DeKok, Irmgard screamed.

DeKok observed the experts moving about in the room. Despite the gruesome circumstances, he was strangely content. At last he had his 'own' team around him. He had liked Tees, the dactyloscopist from the Twenty-third Precinct. He'd even found the coroner from Oldkerk, Dr. Han, a sympathetic young man. In DeKok's perception, however, they were strangers … not the group of people he had worked with for years. He had quietly pulled some strings to work with Bram Weelen, the photographer, and Frans Kruger, the fingerprint expert. Also present was old Dr. Koning and his own team of paramedics. As far as DeKok was concerned, those three and Vledder formed the only team he needed. There was no confusion about who did what, or what jurisdiction prevailed. Regardless of its location, the crime scene was now the sole responsibility of Warmoes Street Station, in casu, DeKok. Once he finished, the inevitable technical team could do what they wanted. At least it would be a team supplied by headquarters, *not* the Twenty-third Precinct.

DeKok reflected as he watched. How many cases had he handled? It must be at least a hundred by now. His was a strange occupation. He hadn't originally been assigned to homicide detail. His first stint was as a uniformed constable. Afterward he had become part of the so-called "Flying Squad," which was solely instituted to handle murders. Until that time there had not been a sufficient number of murders in Amsterdam to worry about a special homicide division. Now the Amsterdam Homicide Division had members spread out over the various precincts.

He looked at Ivo Bildijk and thought about the conversations he had had with the deceased. This time his crafty eloquence had not saved him. Was he the victim of his own almost slavish dedication to his Aunt Isolde? Was there someone who saw the closeness between Ivo and his aunt as a danger? Who was the unknown high-stakes player to whom their liaison was such a threat?

Bram Weelen approached him. The cheerful photographer was in a bad mood. He looked tired, pale with red-rimmed eyes."

"That's the third time this week I've been called out of bed," he said grumpily. He waved with a hand that held a light meter. "This is getting to be carnage—where's the end of it? Anyway how many Bildijk friends and relatives could there be?"

"I'm afraid this is not the last Bildijk to be a target," shrugged DeKok.

"Perhaps you should evacuate them, put them in protective custody. That way they'll have to stop killing each other."

"And you won't be called out of your bed anymore," smiled DeKok.

"No rest for the weary," grumbled Weelen. "They'll just call me for something else."

"There's always that," agreed DeKok.

Bram Weelen took the flash attachment from his camera and re-packed his suitcase.

"Do you insist on having these pictures in the morning?"

DeKok shook his head.

"Take your time. Get a few hours sleep, first. You look like you can use it."

"You ain't kidding," said Weelen with a grateful look. He picked up his suitcase and waved vaguely at the rest of the room. He left.

Dr. Koning patted DeKok on the arm.

"The man is dead," he announced.

"Thank you, doctor," replied DeKok formally.

The aged coroner lifted his greenish Garibaldi head in farewell and, nodding to his assistants, left the room.

After a confirming look at DeKok, who nodded, the morgue attendants approached the corpse. Carefully they lifted the corpse out of the chair and into the body bag. They closed the bag and lifted it onto the stretcher. Once they fastened a few straps, they too, left.

Then DeKok approached Vledder, who was talking to Kruger. DeKok wanted to say something about the geese, still neglected on the lawn. Penny appeared in the door opening, catching his attention. Her bare feet were visible below a soft pink nightgown. She placed her index finger over her lips in the universal sign for silence and then beckoned to DeKok.

DeKok walked softly to the door. She took his hand and pulled him into the corridor. Toward the end in a type of niche, she stopped and looked at DeKok with big, serious eyes.

"I've seen him, Mr. DeKok," she whispered.

"Who, Penny?"

She pointed down the corridor.

"The man who beat Uncle Ivo."

"Are you sure?"

The little one nodded vigorously.

"I saw him go into Uncle Ivo's room."

"Did you recognize him?"

Penny shook her head. Her blonde tresses danced around her face.

"I've never seen him before."

DeKok leaned closer to her.

"Why don't you just stay in bed at night, like your brothers. What can you possibly do at night?"

The little girl gave him a beaming smile. Her whole face lit up.

"I look," she said, "I look at Aunt Isolde when she walks and thinks nobody can see her."

"Walks?"

Penny nodded her head. The tresses again danced around her face.

"Yes, with her cane."

18

Commissaris Buitendam, the tall aristocratic chief of War-moes Street Station, motioned with a graceful, well-manicured hand toward the chair in front of his desk.

"Sit down, DeKok," he said with a voice full of portent. "It's my task to … eh, I have a … I must give you some … ah, some less than pleasant news."

DeKok remained standing.

"I'm listening," he replied curtly.

Buitendam cleared his throat.

"I have to … we must put a stop to your investigations concerning Happy Lake. I, that is, the head of detectives at the Twenty-third Precinct will be in charge going forward. He is a chief inspector, after all."

DeKok had expected anything, but this.

"You're taking me off the case? After you forced it on me?"

Buitendam nodded.

"Three murders in three days, all three happening practically under your eyes … I cannot condone that type of performance. I … eh, I cannot defend it."

DeKok gestured vehemently.

"You have nothing to condone," he screamed. "There's nothing to defend. I have done the best I could and more."

The commissaris made soothing motions with one hand, while the other hand was held up in a defensive gesture.

"We feel the latter is open to interpretation. As a matter of fact, there's some doubt whether your best is good enough. As you will recall, you took on this case with a great deal of reluctance. Your attitude is reflected in the results to date."

With heroic effort DeKok managed to abate the fury that seemed about to posses him.

"Vledder and I have been on the case practically night and day. We left no stone unturned. It is a very complicated case. The motives of those involved are convoluted, to say the least."

"At Happy Lake," interrupted the commissaris, "they are not all so pleased with your performance, either. We discussed their displeasure on an earlier occasion."

"And who are *they,*" demanded DeKok, a dangerous light in his eyes.

"Isolde Bildijk ... she's approached the judge advocate with a pressing request to take you off the case. Mr. Schaap is very sympathetic to Mrs. Bildijk's feelings and opinions. *He* feels more could ..."

It was DeKok's turn to interrupt.

"Mr. Schaap," he said with contempt in his voice. "I've never met a judge advocate who's as sheepish as that one."

Since "schaap" is the Dutch word for *sheep,* DeKok's barb hit hard. The commissaris started to grow splotchy again."

"Again, DeKok, I forbid you to speak like that about a judicial authority."

DeKok barked a short, derisive laugh.

"In your heart you know I'm right," he said angrily. "He's a worthless ... judicial authority, ha, more like a waste of space."

Commissaris Buitendam stood up and pointed at the door. His composure gone, his skin had fully reddened.

"OUT!" he roared.

DeKok stayed where he was and stubbornly shook his head.

"And I've had enough of *that,* too. That is not the way a good chief, a leader, ends a conversation." He sighed deeply, gathering himself. "I know," he continued reasonably. "I'm not very subservient, never have been. I like to be independent ... self-sufficiency has always served me well, so it is difficult for me to depend on anybody. But I do have a request: give me twelve hours."

"No."

"Twelve hours."

"No."

For a few seconds DeKok gave the commissaris a hard, considering look. He had known the chief for years. They had never been friends. Their way of looking at life, their opinions were too far apart. It was not common knowledge, but they had been at the police academy together. Buitendam, primarily a political animal, had quickly risen along the hierarchical ladder. DeKok, a hands-on cop, was stuck in his rank as Inspector. He would never rise higher. Despite their many differences, there was a certain mutual respect, even a certain amount of affection between the two men.

"Twelve hours," repeated DeKok, "and I'll give you the solution of this mystery, dead geese and all."

DeKok felt a strange inner tension. He could not afford any more mistakes, mishaps, or missed communications. The twelve hours he had finally wrested away from Buitendam was the home stretch, his drop deadline. The commissaris would not have the fortitude to resist the diminutive, but

powerful, Judge Advocate Schaap any further. If the commissaris were to give in, DeKok would be dismissed from a case
for the first time in his long career. He could not conceive
of anything more humiliating.

DeKok looked at his watch. More than an hour and
a half ago, he and Vledder had taken up their more or less
strategic position. With distaste he picked up the cell phone
that Vledder had provided. It doubled as a walkie-talkie, one
of a set of four. Vledder had patiently set the instrument for
walkie-talkie mode only. He replaced the tiny beep with a
vibrating warning. All DeKok had to do was listen, or press
a button when he wanted to speak. Apart from Vledder's
phone, two additional units went to young Sergeants Elsberg
and Brink. They were posted, each in his own car, on the
road to Happy Lake. One was on the road leading to Amsterdam, the other, on the road leading to Oldkerk. The gate had
been propped open.

Irmgard's bedroom offered few options for hiding. Vledder and DeKok were underneath the high, old-fashioned
bed. DeKok glanced at Vledder and heard steady, unhurried
breathing. Vledder was tense, but relaxed. The room had been
left almost dark, but there was enough light to distinguish
furniture and colors. A bright red nightgown, belonging to
Irmgard, had been draped over a chair; the hem was just visible next to one of the legs. They had an unobstructed view
of the door.

DeKok had used all his persuasion to get Irmgard's
cooperation. She was his only chance. Irmgard looked for
ways out—she stalled with one excuse or another. She
wanted to consult her husband, but he could not been
reached. She wanted to wait until she could reach him,
before agreeing. DeKok had explained patiently how she

was in grave danger as long as the murderer had not been caught. In the end she agreed.

DeKok sighed deeply, but silently. He felt his pulse and found it calm and steady. He knew more or less what would happen, but could not be absolutely sure. He sneaked another peek at his watch. Time seemed to stand still. Every minute seemed an eternity.

Suddenly they heard soft footsteps in the corridor outside the bedroom. The door of the room opened slowly.

DeKok saw the legs of dark trousers and what looked like cowboy boots. The heels were elevated. Vledder and DeKok held their breath. The boots stopped behind the chair. There was a sudden movement, the whistling of air, followed by the sound of an impact. A blonde wig was thrown across the room and a dented, wood head rolled over the brightly colored carpet.

Later DeKok remembered what happened then as a slow-motion picture. The two inspectors emerged from underneath the bed.

Overwhelmed and bewildered, Igor Stablinsky looked at them as if he had seen ghosts. He stood transfixed, but the trance lasted only a second. He pirouetted swiftly and fled. Before Vledder and DeKok could reach the door, Igor had closed and locked it.

Vledder smashed a shoulder into the door, but the door did not give an inch.

DeKok shook his head in disgust and pressed the button on the phone in his hand. He barked a number of commands, while Vledder took a chair and smashed the window. He took a quick look at the glass shards remaining in the frame. With a rapid movement he swept the chair across the remaining shards. He tossed the chair behind him and jumped out of the window. DeKok followed close behind.

They ran through the garden around the house. When they reached the front of the house, they saw a car parked in front of the steps leading to the front door. It was a large, dark vehicle.

Isolde Bildijk stood next to the open rear door, leaning on a stick. Igor was in the process of helping her into the car. He slammed the rear door of the vehicle behind Isolde, ran around to the driver's seat, and slid behind the wheel. The engine caught immediately, and the car sped away, spewing a fountain of gravel behind it.

Vledder pulled his service weapon. DeKok said nothing, but ran after the disappearing car. He counted on Vledder's good sense not to fire the pistol at the fleeing car. Outside of the rapidly increasing distance, steadying for an accurate shot would have been out of the question. Running distances and shooting don't mix, except in Hollywood.

Igor swiftly increased speed. He had almost reached the gate when two police cars turned into the gate, almost side by side. The lights on top of the cars were flashing and their high beams blinded everyone in their path.

Igor, too, lost his vision for a moment. Instinctively he turned the wheel and crossed the lawn, headed straight for the pile of dead geese. The impact and the slippery surface caused the vehicle to tip over on its side. A second bump rolled the car on its roof. The car progressed a few more feet upside down, stopping against an immense oak with an impact that shook leaves off the tree.

DeKok had watched with consternation. He kept running in his strange duck gait. He had seen Isolde Bildijk thrown from the car. Her body landed close to the now scattered heap of dead geese. Her cane was nearby. DeKok knelt next to the body. Isolde's eyes were closed, but she was still breathing. Quickly DeKok examined the body. His hands carefully, but thoroughly searched for blood, or fractures, but he could find no obvious trauma.

Suddenly, in the reflected glare of the police headlights, DeKok noticed the approach of a pair of high-heeled boots. He looked up.

Igor Stablinsky paused a moment to pick up the discarded cane and hefted it in his right hand.

DeKok held his eyes on Igor. The old inspector was panting and half crouched down. He forced his breathing to be normal and then pulled his mouth into an ugly grin.

"You wouldn't dare, Igor. Not this way. Once a coward, always a coward—you don't have the guts!

Behind him, DeKok heard rapid footsteps on the gravel.

"Mr. DeKok ... Mr. DeKok!"

DeKok heard Penny's voice and turned around. At the same time he realized his mistake. He had turned his back on Igor. He dropped flat to the ground.

A shot went off and the cane fell from Igor's hand. With a grotesque gesture Stablinsky threw both arms high in the air before collapsing.

DeKok kneeled on one knee. Crying, little Penny flew into his arms. The old inspector closed his eyes for a moment and tried to control his emotions.

"What ... what's the matter, honey?"

His voice trembled just a little.

The little girl pointed at Igor's corpse.

"That man ... that's the man who beat Uncle Ivo."

19

DeKok later invited Vledder and the two young detective-sergeants, Elsberg and Brink, for a cozy evening at his home. He was well aware that the gruesome end on the Happy Lake estate had left unanswered questions.

During that desperate end game, in fact, Elsberg and Brink confided they would love to know *what* exactly was happening. It was the first time the two young men had been present at the end of one of DeKok's cases. Vledder, of course, knew most of the details from the report he had prepared for the commissaris. But some details had been left out. DeKok had added those verbally when he presented the report to Buitendam.

The gray sleuth sank down in his leather club chair. He still felt the tension of the last few days in his bones. It seemed to last longer than on previous occasions. It seemed to abate much slower as well. He had succeeded but, literally, at the last minute.

He looked at the young people surrounding him and wondered how much longer he would be able to put up with the mental and physical stresses of his demanding job.

His mind wandered toward Little Lowee and a faint smile flashed across his wide face. Only this morning the diminutive, scrappy barkeeper had sent over a splendid bottle of cognac from his own hidden cache. Apparently word had spread via the underworld grapevine to Lowee's rather less savory circles. There was a brief note with the bottle. 'Proost ... to a long life, but not so long for Igor.' The note was in Lowee's almost indecipherable scribble. It was a harsh sentiment, but DeKok understood Lowee. In his own way, he did not just celebrate Igor's death, but lauded DeKok's survival.

DeKok rose from his chair and picked up Lowee's bottle of cognac. With keen anticipation he filled the wide, deep snifters and served his guests.

Mrs. DeKok appeared from the kitchen with platters heaped high with a variety of delicacies. The Dutch seldom drink without eating, and have filled entire cookbooks with recipes for just that purpose. The variety of food the Dutch call "bitter food" would put a smorgasbord to shame. It is called "bitter" food, because the Dutch National drink, Jenever, is commonly called a 'bitter.' Mrs. DeKok was a culinary genius, who performed magic in the kitchen. Vledder, who knew her reputation well, cast greedy eyes over the mouthwatering display.

Mrs. DeKok arranged the platters on a sideboard, while she gave Vledder an admiring smile.

"I heard the whole story," she said. "You saved my husband's life."

The young inspector shrugged shyly.

"Now I'm beginning to understand why DeKok never wants to carry a weapon and why he's always insisting that I never use one. My fingers are sore and bruised from report writing ... was it necessary to shoot the victim fatally ... what other means were at your disposal ... was the life of your colleague really in danger?" He shook his head in mock despair. "And then the interviews at headquarters and in our own station. It was all the way over the top."

He paused for a moment and made a movement toward the trays with food. Then he controlled the urge to stuff himself.

"I really wonder about those guys at headquarters," he continued. "Igor Stablinsky was probably the most dangerous person we've encountered in years. There's clear evidence of at least two murders on his conscience—at the time, probably three more. As the officer involved, I was expected to make a split-second decision to fire or not. I regret I had to take a life, but I still don't see how I could have acted otherwise."

DeKok nodded agreement.

"I share some of the responsibility," admitted DeKok. "I should not have turned my back on him when Penny came running toward me. If Dick had not acted," he added cynically, "this party would have been a wake, with me as the guest of honor. The old lady's cane was filled with lead."

"With lead ... but why?" asked Brink.

"Old Willem did that for her when she complained about being a poor defenseless invalid in a large, unguarded house. She was on about having no means of protecting herself." He grinned sadly. "In reality, she already intended to use the stick to wipe out her nephews and her niece."

Vledder had not known that.

"Really, was that her plan?"

"Yes," answered DeKok. "I've spent quite a few hours with her in the hospital. She was very calm, and collected. She also did not hold anything back. Very forthcoming."

Vledder gave him an intent look.

"Does she know Igor is dead?"

DeKok closed his eyes, a painful look on his face.

"I debated telling her, but to my surprise, she hardly reacted at all. Actually, she registered relief, as if she had been freed from a burden."

Mrs. DeKok could not let that go by unchallenged.

"But he was her son!" she exclaimed.

"Agreed," answered DeKok, "but a son who brought her little joy."

A silence fell, finally broken by Elsberg.

"But I don't understand it all. What was that woman after? And who is this Igor and how is he connected to it all?"

DeKok smiled tolerantly.

"I understand," he said, "but before we go any further. Let's have a sip of cognac and ..." he pointed at the trays, "that smells delicious."

Mrs. DeKok took a small plate and loaded a variety of snacks for her husband. The three young men were making their selections as well, guided by Vledder who was familiar with the delicacies Mrs. DeKok provided. The two sergeants filled their plates according to Vledder's directions. Vledder was trying to decide between two kinds of tiny cream puffs. One kind was filled with a delicate fish ragout and the other kind was filled with an aromatic meat ragout. In the end he took a generous helping of both. He added a few slices of pickled herring and several varieties of cheese. Ruefully he looked as his filled plate, but than realized he could go back for seconds, or thirds, or more.

The three young men reseated themselves while DeKok bit with relish into a croquette, liberally covered by spicy mustard. Mrs. DeKok smiled benignly at the men, but did not eat anything herself. She sipped at her sherry and looked at DeKok with a meaningful glance.

"Oh, yes," said DeKok, hastily swallowing the last of his croquette and taking a swallow from his cognac. "Vledder, too was on the wrong trail for a while. I was not, because I was not on any trail ... I was just puzzled."

"DeKok!" warned his wife.

"All right ... al right ... . Originally Vledder thought, and I did not disagree with him, that the two nephews, Ivo and Izaak, and the niece, Irmgard, were after each other in order to gain the inheritance from their Aunt Isolde. We started to look at the events at Happy Lake in that light and drew the wrong conclusions ... despite my doubt about the motives, I could not think of any other possibilities. It was not until after our conversation with Uncle Immanuel, in Bussum, that I started to understand what *could* have happened."

"Please allow me to observe," said Brink diffidently with a heavy Rotterdam accent, "that at this point it's all Greek to me."

"You're right, Johnny," conceded DeKok. He picked up his glass and took another swallow. "I'll try to sketch in the background as concise and as complete as possible. If there are still any questions after that, I'll answer them as best as I can."

DeKok placed his glass next to the small plate with food on the little table next to his chair. With a resolute gesture he turned away from the temptations and faced his audience.

"Once upon a time ..." he began, then laughed sourly. "It's not a nice fairy tale ... but, then, fairy tales are never very nice."

"DeKok!" warned his wife again.

"Yes," continued DeKok, "once upon a time, not so long ago, there was man called Izaak Bildijk. He earned a fortune young, married, and had four sons. The first son was called Ignatius, the next one was called Iwert, the third was Immanuel, and the fourth son was Ilja. Izaak Bildijk bought the Happy Lake estate to settle down and raise his family. At his death, he left the entire estate to his eldest son, Ignatius. The estate included the house and all its surrounding lands.

In addition to the large garden, there were a great number of acres of farmland under lease to neighboring farmers."

"So, Ignatius was the lucky heir," remarked Elsberg.

"Exactly," continued DeKok. "Ignatius married in due course. The happy couple produced a daughter, whom they called Isolde. Rather than a blessing, Isolde became a curse to her parents. She was, what's called a 'bad seed.' Promiscuous in her early teens, by eighteen she met a Polish violinist in Amsterdam. This gypsy musician, Peter Stablinsky, inveigled her to abandon her life and family in Amsterdam to accompany him on his tours of Europe. Once she discovered she was pregnant, she demanded he marry her. They married and stayed for a time in Gdansk, where the child was born. The child they named Igor. Isolde and Peter were not finished wandering. They left Igor with his Polish grandparents in Gdansk, rather than be burdened with a baby boy. Their actions did not serve them any better than they served the child. Without an anchor or responsibilities, the couple broke up. Russia was the end of the line—they officially divorced there. Isolde went back home, to Holland."

DeKok paused and gave his wife a plaintive look. She handed him the bottle of cognac and he poured himself a generous measure. He held up the bottle, looking at his guests in an inviting manner. They all hastened to get a refill. When they had all settled back in their chairs Mrs. DeKok asked a question.

"What about the child?" she wanted to know.

"Igor stayed with the grandparents in Gdansk. Isolde never gave herself a chance to develop a nurturing side, assuming she had one."

"That's incredible."

"During her long absence," DeKok went on, "things had

changed at Happy Lake. Isolde's parents had died and the estate had reverted to the second son, Iwert." DeKok raised an index finger in the air. "Now it gets complicated," he warned. "Isolde's uncle, Iwert, who had inherited the estate in his turn, was not married. Isolde challenged the inheritance, contending she should have inherited the estate of her parents. In fact, she had a valid claim. But her very rich Uncle Immanuel, Iwert's brother, arranged for them *both* to stay at Happy Lake. In order to quell the rumors, Isolde decided to marry Iwert."

"But that was incest," protested Elsberg.

"Yes, but one can marry a blood relative with a special dispensation from the Crown. Historically, only the aristocracy applied for such a dispensation, in order to preserve a particular bloodline. It has always been, however, available to all citizens. And the Bildijk family had enough influence to get it approved in record time."

"So, she married her uncle, the brother of her father."

"Yes," answered DeKok. "And thereby she achieved a double status. She remained the niece of her rich uncle Immanuel, but at the same time she was the 'aunt' of her cousins, Ivo, Izaak, and Irmgard ... the children of her youngest uncle, Izaak."

"And there's where I went wrong," interrupted Vledder. "Just like Ilja's children, I saw Isolde as just an 'aunt,' the widow of their uncle Iwert."

DeKok encouraged him by lifting his glass in salute.

"Exactly," he confirmed, "just like you ... like all of us, they forgot or did not know Isolde was an equal heir of their uncle, Immanuel."

"Aha," exclaimed Brink suddenly. "Now, I see. If Isolde killed her cousins, she would be the only heir left of Immanuel's fortune."

DeKok rubbed his chin.

"Greed is often the primary motivation for murder," he said thoughtfully.

Elsberg gestured impatiently.

"But what about Igor, how does he fit in?"

DeKok shook his head.

"At first, he did not fit in at all. When his father died, relatively young, he stayed with his grandparents, who merely told him that his mother was Isolde Bildijk of the Netherlands, the daughter of a rich family. At first Igor spoke only Polish and German, but he studied Dutch and when he was sure enough of himself, he traveled to Happy Lake and presented himself to his mother. That was the day that Isolde's paralysis first manifested itself. She made him swear never to come to Happy Lake during the day and paid him whatever he asked. And that was a lot … she had to sell the leased lands and took several mortgages on the rest of the estate in order to satisfy Igor's demands. Finally she could no longer pay her son. And although she lived very frugally, the debts piled up. The only one who knew was Willem, the gardener. His meager wages had not been paid for a year. But he was very attached to Isolde, stayed on, and did whatever she wanted. She used him outrageously."

He paused and nibbled on some of the food. Then he drained his glass and looked around for the bottle.

"No," said his wife. "Finish what you started, first."

DeKok smiled tenderly.

"Very well," he picked up his narrative. "When Isolde's debts kept increasing, she thought of her uncle Immanuel and the share of her inheritance. Before anything else, she wanted to hold on to Happy Lake and restore the estate to its former glory. She realized that Immanuel's inheritance, if it had to be shared, would be insufficient."

"And that's when she decided to wipe out the competition," grinned Brink.

"It's no laughing matter," answered DeKok. "It's rather sad. In order to remove the other heirs, she needed them nearby. Her disability left her no other option. She shrewdly badgered the Twenty-third Precinct with tales of terror. She demanded protection. She drew the family in by telling them she was being threatened. As proof she wrote threatening letters to herself and asked Willem to mail them from Oldkerk."

"What," exclaimed Vledder, "Willem knew all the time?"

"Yes, Willem knew a lot. He knew all about her debts. He knew there were times she could get around very well without her wheelchair. Isolde realized the danger Willem posed. He would see through her plan as no one else would. He knew the background and the issues involved. At first she wanted to kill him, but then thought of a better idea. She poisoned the geese and then tried to have me arrest Willem for destruction of property, as well as for writing the threatening letters she had sent herself."

"She was ruthless," remarked Mrs. DeKok, condemnation in her voice.

"Indeed," agreed DeKok with his wife. "To resume ... when I refused to arrest the gardener, she grew desperate. The gardener *had* to disappear from the scene before she could start killing her family. The cousins had already arrived after her alarming pleas for assistance. The very first night they were all in the house, she sneaked up to the coach house and killed the old man with her cane. It was reinforced with lead, as you'll remember."

"In retrospect," mused Vledder, "we should have arrested him. He might still be alive." He shrugged apologetically.

"But who could know the evil that was to come."

"Yes," said DeKok with regret in his voice. "I did not arrest him because I was convinced of his innocence. There is no consolation in being right; the death of that old man touched me deeply. I liked him and I admired his loyalty, however misplaced, to Isolde. Early on, my instinct was that there were a lot of secrets to be discovered between those two."

Brink was getting impatient.

"What else happened? Surely, that's not all."

"No," admitted DeKok. "As formidable as Isolde was, she couldn't control everything. Imagine her dread when she discovered Igor had escaped from custody. She knew his arrest was for at least one murder. She'd counted on his being out of circulation for some time to come. Igor contacted her immediately after his release, demanding money to escape from the Netherlands. Isolde told him once again she had no money and was unable to help him … until Uncle Immanuel had died. But she convinced Igor to wait with that job, until the task at Happy Lake had been completed."

Vledder explained to Elsberg and Brink.

"That's how it happened. Someone spotted Igor in Bussum. His uncle saw Igor around the neighborhood. He must have been casing the joint."

"Yes, yes," said DeKok, now apparently impatient to finish up. "But something else unexpected happened. Izaak, the nephew, or cousin, depending on your point of view, was richly endowed with the Bildijk flaws of avarice and viciousness. He was looking to hire a killer, a person who could, and would, murder his Aunt Isolde. He stumbled into Igor. It was pure coincidence. He had read about Igor in the newspapers. The combination was too tempting. After Izaak phoned Igor to plan his aunt's demise, Igor immediately called his mother and told her about Izaak's plan. Isolde took no half measures. She waited for Izaak to come home and killed him."

"So, that was her second murder," counted Elsberg.

"And her last," replied DeKok. "Igor assured her he was better equipped to take care of the other victims. It was a desperation move on his part. It was matter of all or nothing. He was being hunted for at least one murder already. A few more or less made no difference to him. Also, he promised Isolde he would confess to the murders of Willem and Izaak, in the event of his arrest. The apple didn't fall far from the tree—she copied his style. Isolde accepted her son's plan. The next night she let him into the house."

"And Igor killed Ivo," said Elsberg.

DeKok paused and looked at the bottle. This time his wife relented and handed the bottle to her husband. With a grateful smile he poured himself another glass and then passed the bottle around. Only Vledder had another helping.

"Finish your tale, please," said Mrs. DeKok. "I'll go make coffee." She pointed at the buffet. "And I would be disappointed if all that food went to waste. The three young men and her husband assured her that would be unlikely. Mrs. DeKok disappeared in the kitchen.

"There's not much left to tell," said DeKok. "During our crazy drive from Bussum to Happy Lake, it started to come together. It was too late for Ivo, but I knew that Irmgard would be the next victim. I contacted her and explained the situation. She moved into the room with her eldest son. Later that night she let Vledder and me into the house via the French doors in what had been Izaak's room. We brought a wig and a store dummy's head, to set the scene. We propped the head in the chair and draped one of Irmgard's nightgowns around the chair. Next we waited underneath the bed." DeKok spread his arms wide. "The rest all of you know already."

There was long silence while they nibbled the food and sipped from their drinks. Mrs. DeKok returned with the coffee. Vledder hastened to help her with the tray.

"Is Isolde going to recover?" asked DeKok's wife.

"Her injuries are relatively slight. A lot of bruises, but no internal damage."

"And then what"

DeKok smiled sadly.

"That's up to the judge." He poured himself another glass of cognac, while the young men accepted cups of coffee and refilled their plates. The conversation became more general and slowly the horrors of Happy Lake retreated into the background.

Late that night, when the younger men had left, DeKok sank back in his chair. His wife handed him a cup of coffee.

"This time I almost lost you," she said.

Her husband smiled.

"All weeds grow apace," he joked complacently.

He took an envelope from his pocket.

"I received a letter," he said, as he pulled a sheet out of the crumpled envelope. He read aloud:

> *Dear Mr. DeKok:*
> *I'm sorry it's all over. I thought it was rather exciting at Happy Lake. I also hope you never turn your back on me. But if you do, don't be afraid, I'm a Miller, not a Bildijk.*
> *—Penny*

DeKok and The Grinning Strangler

Inspector DeKok (Homicide) held forth in the old, renowned police station at Warmoes Street in the older, more renowned city of Amsterdam. The senior inspector pulled a report from his desk drawer. He looked at the report, annoyance on his face. Then he tossed it back into the drawer, slamming the drawer back in the closed position. He rose from his chair and walked over to the window of the long, narrow detective room. He paused at the window, hands behind his back. Softly he rocked back and forth on the balls of his feet.

Dick Vledder, his young colleague and friend, came to stand next to the old man. He eyed DeKok from the side.

"What's the matter, don't feel up to it, or just bored with it?"

"Both," growled DeKok. "Mostly I feel you spend too much time on that computer, writing reports I don't want to read. Once I do read them, they just end up in some file."

"Do you want to change the law?"

DeKok shook his head.

"No, but every inspector should have a secretary."

"Right," laughed Vledder happily. "I'm ready to interview. I'd like a good-looking, leggy female."

DeKok ignored the remark.

"What we need is more freedom to act. We should not be forced to write down every little thing that happens. Bah, I can't even blow my own nose without having to write a report about it. The lawyers are always talking about illegally obtained evidence and more of that nonsense. Evidence is evidence, no more, no less ... as long as we don't obtain it by torture."

The gray sleuth waved a hand toward the rooftops of Amsterdam.

"Out there," he continued, "at the end of the alley is *Ons Lieve Heer op Solder* (Our Dear Lord in the Attic), by all accounts the most beautiful and sweetest museum in Amsterdam. I can get there from here, but only by means of an alley named for Heintje Hook. Hook was a savage pirate of his day, greatly feared because of his brutality." He spread his arms wide. "There's some kind of symbolic meaning in all that."

"What sort of symbolic meaning?"

"It is an allegory relating to our job," DeKok responded. "If our goal is to catch criminals we must be free to follow strange paths, if and when it becomes necessary."

"I don't get your meaning."

"Years ago, before your time," sighed DeKok, "I was in charge of a burglary case. It involved breaking and entering the warehouse of a furrier. The job was beautiful, perfectly executed. There was no vandalism, no violence, just attention to detail and efficiency. In those days there was a dying breed of burglars, men who took pride in their work. They were masters of their craft and of their domain."

"So?"

"I found out from the furrier only the most expensive furs had been stolen. The thief had lifted just the sables, the finest minks. This was a very selective burglar. The furrier's inventory included hundreds of gorgeous, less valuable furs. Those had been left untouched."

"So the perpetrator must have been another furrier?" guessed Vledder.

"No. After some thought, I knew of only one local man. This was someone who had the necessary skills and knowledge to make a quick, clean entry. It was his trademark. Another trademark was his acquisition of knowledge. He would either have the expertise or would acquire it to make an exquisite, informed selection. The man was Handy Henkie. I decided to call on him and propose he just return the furs to me. Of course the confrontation didn't go so smoothly. He laughed in my face and demanded evidence."

"And you did not have it."

"No, I did not have a shred of evidence. But I took him to the station with me for an interrogation. It was useless. Henkie kept demanding I prove my case. Eventually I returned him to the cell and thought long and hard."

"What did you come up with?"

"I had an idea. I called the owner of the warehouse and asked him to deliver a selection of fur coats, in the same quantity and of the same quality as those he had lost. He delivered them the same afternoon. Right here in this room, I shoved a couple of tables together and tossed the furs in a heap on the tables. Then I took Handy Henkie out of his cell and showed him the furs. 'Well, what do you have to say for yourself?' I asked. 'Holy shit,' said Henkie, 'you found them.'"

Vledder laughed heartily.

DeKok nodded with quiet satisfaction.

"But in Court," DeKok continued, with a tinge of bitterness, "Henkie's lawyer exploded, mostly for the benefit of the jury. He ranted on about my use of what he termed 'illegal and unauthorized means' in getting the confession."

"What did Henkie say?"

DeKok smiled.

"Henkie thought is was a good joke, although the joke was on him. We became friends. When he had done his time, he said he wanted to make an honest living. I helped him get a job as a tool-and-dye maker. He still works for the same employer, his boss and co-workers value him for the high quality of his work. Apparently he never lost his attention to detail."

The phone on DeKok's desk rang. Vledder reached over and lifted the receiver. DeKok watched as Vledder's face became grave.

"What's the matter?" asked DeKok as Vledder replaced the receiver.

"They found a young prostitute."

"Dead?"

Vledder nodded.

"That's why they called us. It seems she's been strangled."

Black Annie was naked and supine on the bed in her room. Her left leg was partly pulled up. Her brown eyes in her slightly swollen face were wide open. A man's silk necktie was around her neck ... red and with a unique design.

DeKok leaned over the dead body and studied the clearly visible strangulation striations. The old sleuth had seen a lot of strangulations in his long career. He had attended the autopsies and he knew that the cartilage in the young neck was crushed.

He straightened out and pointed at a used condom next to the bed. He beckoned Vledder.

"Make sure we get pictures of everything and make sure that they take this condom to the lab. It could yield more than DNA evidence. Perhaps they'll discover some pubic hair, and forensics can give a rapid turnaround on blood type."

He turned toward the corpse.

"And make sure they're careful with that tie. I don't want it touched by anyone. Tell the crime scene people to use tweezers, or a surgical clamp, to remove it. I want it bagged, separate from everything. We might have to use a dog to sniff out the owner."

"You're leaving?" asked Vledder.

DeKok pointed upstairs.

"I'm going to have a chat with Limburger Lena. She owns the place."

He took a last look around the room and a pitying look came into his eyes as he looked at the dead face. Then he walked out.

Limburger Lena was distressed. Her face was pale and her eyes were rimmed in red when DeKok entered her room. When she saw him she stood up and put away a small handkerchief.

"It must have been that rich guy," she blurted out. "Today is Friday. And he comes every Friday around the same time to visit Annie."

"Who is he?"

"A john … wants you to know he's rich; he flashes the designer labels and big jewelry. Drives a big, late-model car. He's one of Annie's regulars. He's been here every Friday for several weeks."

"What about today?"

She shook her head.

"No, not today ... that is," she hesitated, "I didn't notice. I had other things on my mind."

"What kind of car does this rich john drive?"

"I don't know. I can't tell them apart." She shuffled over to the mantelpiece. "But I *do* have his tag number. Here it is, I wrote it down a few weeks ago."

"Why?"

"Something just wasn't right about him. I never liked him."

DeKok took the piece of paper. It was a blank strip torn from a newspaper. He looked at the number.

"May I use your phone?" he asked.

By the time DeKok came back downstairs, two morgue attendants were carrying the young woman's body down the steep stairs. They shoved the stretcher into the back of their van, closed the doors, and drove away.

DeKok walked over to Vledder.

"Have they all been here?"

"And gone," confirmed Vledder. "Here's the necktie." He handed DeKok a plastic bag.

From Limburger Lena's establishment, they retraced their steps to the station house. A small army of those in need of sexual release, or who thought they were, paraded along the lighted windows. As usual, it was busy in front of the windows of the sex shops. There were always long rows of men waiting for the peep shows. The loss of one of their own never even slowed business in the Quarter. If anyone missed or mourned Black Annie, their grief wouldn't interfere with profits.

When they arrived at the station, DeKok stopped near the desk sergeant. He handed a piece of paper to Vledder.

"Arrest that man."

Vledder read out loud.

"Gerardus Aardenburg." He looked at DeKok.

"Is that the killer?"

"For now he's a person of interest."

Limburger Lena had been right. Gerardus Aardenburg had been left to cool his heels in the cells for several hours, but he still made a bold, flashy impression. DeKok observed him closely. He saw a round face, gleaming with sweat and oil. His green eyes were almost hidden behind red, round cheeks. "Pig eyes," thought DeKok.

"Yeah," gestured Aardenburg. "I knew the whore. So what? You have no right to detain me. I'm innocent. I didn't kill her."

"But you went there every Friday?"

"Sure, for a few weeks." Again he shrugged his shoulders, as if to profess his innocence. "But I didn't go there today. Besides, I have an alibi."

DeKok rubbed the bridge of his nose with his little finger. Then he looked at his finger for a long moment as if he had never seen it before.

"Anyone can buy an alibi," he said finally, thoughtfully. "All it takes is cash. You aren't keeping a low profile—it seems to me you have the resources."

Aardenburg shook his head.

"I'm not saying another word, not until my lawyer is here."

DeKok nodded resignedly. He tried a few more times to elicit a response. When Aardenburg refused to say anything, other than to repeat his request for a lawyer, he had the man taken back to his cell. DeKok remained staring into the distance. Then he beckoned Vledder.

"I had hoped for a ready confession," he said. "But I don't see that confession forthcoming. We don't really have a legal leg to stand on. Call the watch commander and have him get evidence to return Aardenburg's personal effects. As soon as processing is complete, we'll have to release him."

DeKok waited for Vledder to complete the call and then he asked the young man to follow him. The two hustled down the stairs and out of the station. They stopped on the corner of the alley.

"What are we doing here?" Vledder wanted to know.

"We wait for Aardenburg to come out of the station."

"And then what?"

"I'm curious to see if he's wearing a necktie."

"He was wearing a necktie when I arrested him," said Vledder.

"They boxed it up, along with his shoe laces, his belt, and other possessions when they frisked him. So, why shouldn't he be wearing a necktie?"

"This is the tie he was wearing when you arrested him."

Vledder looked at the garment.

"That's right," he confirmed, puzzlement in his voice.

Aardenburg left the station house. There was a satisfied grin on his greasy face. With a familiar gesture, he adjusted his necktie as he surveyed the street.

Vledder looked at the tie in DeKok's hand.

"But he's wearing a tie again," he wondered.

A faint smile played around DeKok's lips.

"Arrest him again," he said calmly. "Now he's wearing the tie that was used to strangle Annie. I exchanged them after he was led to the cells. Both his ties. He just never noticed the difference."

DeKok and Murder By Melody

by Baantjer

"Death is entitled to our respect," says Inspector DeKok who finds himself once again amidst dark dealings. A triple murder in the Amsterdam Concert Gebouw has him unveiling the truth behind two dead ex-junkies and their housekeeper.

"DeKok's maverick personality certainly makes him a compassionate judge of other outsiders and an astute analyst of antisocial behavior."

—*The New York Times Book Review*

"DeKok is a careful, compassionate policeman in the tradition of Maigret; crime fans will enjoy this …"

—*Library Journal*

"It's easy to understand the appeal of Amsterdam police detective DeKok."

—*The Los Angeles Times*

0-9725776-9-6

speck

Bullets

by Steve Brewer

When a contract killer bumps off a high roller in a Las Vegas casino, a tangle of romance, gambling, and gunplay follows. The killer, Lily Marsden, is a mysterious and cold woman who is a true professional. But soon, the casino owner, his henchmen, and the victim's two brothers are on Lily's trail.

Former Chicago cop Joe Riley is pursuing Lily, too. She cost him his job as a homicide investigator when suspicion of a bookie's murder fell on him. Joe is certain Lily killed the bookie, and he's tracked her across the country to Vegas.

Throw in some local cops, a playboy, a new widow, a rug merchant, a harridan, and a couple of idiot gamblers named Delbert and Mookie, and the mixture soon boils with intrigue and murder. Add a dash of romance as a strange magnetism develops between Lily and Joe, dust the whole concoction with Steve Brewer's trademark humor, and you end up with *Bullets*—a crime novel you won't soon forget.

0-9725776-7-X

No Laughing Matter

by Peter Guttridge

Tom Sharpe meets Raymond Chandler in *No Laughing Matter* a humorous and brilliant debut that will keep readers on a knife's edge of suspense until the bittersweet end.

When a naked woman flashes past Nick Madrid's hotel window, it's quite a surprise. For Nick's room is on the fourteenth floor, and the hotel doesn't have an outside elevator. The management is horrified when Cissie Parker lands in the swimming pool—not only is she killed, but she makes a real mess of the shallow end.

In Montreal for the Just For Laughs festival, Nick, a journalist who prefers practicing yoga to interviewing the stars, turns gumshoe to answer the question: did she fall or was she pushed? The trail leads first to the mean streets of Edinburgh and then to Los Angeles, where the truth lurks among the dark secrets of Hollywood.

0-9725776-4-5

speck

A Ghost of a Chance

by Peter Guttridge

Nick Madrid isn't exactly thrilled when his best friend in journalism—OK, his *only* friend in journalism—the "Bitch of the Broadsheets", Bridget Frost, commissions him to spend a night in a haunted place on the Sussex Downs and live to tell the tale. Especially as living to tell the tale isn't made an urgent priority.

But Nick stumbles on a hotter story when he discovers a dead man hanging upside down from an ancient oak. Why was he killed? Is there a connection to the nearby New Age conference center? Or to *The Great Beast*, the Hollywood movie about Aleister Crowley, filming down in Brighton?

New Age meets The Old Religion as Nick is bothered, bewildered, but not necessarily bewitched by pagans, satanists and a host of assorted metaphysicians. Séances, sabbats, a horse-ride from hell and a kick-boxing zebra all come Nick's way as he obstinately tracks a treasure once in the possession of Crowley.

0-9725776-8-8

For a comp

Riverton Branch Library
1600 Forest Ave.
Portland, Maine 04103
(207)797-2915

ontact us

speck press
po box 102004
denver, co 80250, usa
e: books@speckpress.com
t: 800-996-9783
f: 303-756-8011

All of our

	DATE DUE		

er.